MORIARTY
PARADIGM

I0518953

BASED UPON THE STORIES AND CHARACTERS CREATED BY
SIR ARTHUR CONAN DOYLE

# THE LAVENDER MEN

BY ADEM ROLFE

Fringeworks

*For*
*Arthur, Herbert and Uncle Terrance*
*standing on the shoulders of giants*

*First Published in Great Britain in 2015 by*
FRINGEWORKS LTD

ISBN: 978-1-909573-20-8
Copyright © 2015 Fringeworks Ltd

Cover Art and Design: Martin Reimann
Cover Format: David R Shires/TheImageDesign

# CONTENTS

# FOREWORD

Despite the fact that Sherlock Holmes found fame as the star of the first modern detective serial, it is as the inspiration for the pulp heroes that followed that he should perhaps be remembered for. In the first instance there were the copyright-breaching continuations of his adventures overseas, which spawned the birth of Harry Dickson, the American Sherlock Holmes. It started in 1907 when a German magazine called *Detective Sherlock Holmes und seine welt berühmten abenteuer* (Sherlock Holmes and his World Famous Adventures) started to tell new stories not approved by Conan Doyle. A change of name (to *Aus dem Geheimakten des Weltdetektivs*— From the Secret Files of the King of Detectives) also saw a change of focus, seeing Sherlock Holmes take on a new sidekick. Out went Watson, and in came a young man called Harry Taxon. With a variety of spin-offs into Dutch, Belgian, French, Australian and American magazines, young Taxon mutated from a Baker Street Irregular who grew up to fill Watson's shoes into the Australian Allan Dickson and the American Harry Dickson, both of whom replaced Holmes as the lead detective. In France the crown of the King of Detectives passed to the cinematic detective, Chantecoq, while other Holmes clones began to emerge else where. In England he was *Sexton Blake, Detective*, an 1893 Holmes clone known throughout his publishing history as the poor man's Sherlock Holmes. Indeed when Blake rights became an issue for his publishers in 1979 he briefly became known as Victor Drago. Another detective in the Holmes mould was Sax Rohmer's Sir Denis Nayland-Smith who, from 1913 until 1959, devoted his retirement to combating that most evil of criminal geniuses, Dr Fu Manchu. British detectives exploded into popular literature, from Buchan's Richard Hannay and Sapper's Bulldog Drummond to Dick Barton, Special Agent and the many two fisted detectives that succeeded them.

In America meanwhile, the faux Holmeses were everywhere—too many to mention or to credit— although the most famous pastiche detectives were Nick Carter, who started life as a Victorian detective in 1886 and survived through film noir to be come a more Bondian hero in the 1960s, and August Derleth's Solar

Pons, who went on to star in more stories than Doyle had written of Holmes. The rise of pulp adventure and film noir soon saw Holmes challenged by heroes often inspired by—but more clearly differentiated from—the great detective.

While Holmes himself never fell from the public eye, his arch-nemesis, Professor James Moriarty, inspired the archetypical supervillain. While Hornung's Raffles—the anti-Holmes—and the French Arsene Lupin pitched the idea of affable villains, it among the likes of Grant Allen's Colonel Clay, Boothby's Dr Nikola and of course Sax Rohmer's Dr Fu Manchu that audiences found their favourites. The criminal mastermind became the staple of adventure fiction (none more so than in the adventures of James Bond) and it is perhaps ironic that, by the 1980s, the man asked to continue the adventures of 007, John Gardner, was similarly commissioned to continue the adventures of James Moriarty.

It is as much to these pulp successors to Sherlock Holmes, and to the journey that they have made, that the Moriarty paradigm owes its existence.

ADRIAN MIDDLETON, 2015
Birmingham, West Midlands

# I. Military Ordnance

While my military career remains little more than a footnote in a very lengthy volume about the History of the Second Afghan War, it must be said that my survival was entirely down to the actions of my only surviving orderly, Private Alexander Murray. We had, I recall, been readying our equipment aboard the Keane, a relief aerostat that had been fitted out as a mobile field hospital capable of treating the injured whilst ferrying them to the nearest fort.

We busied ourselves by preparing for the anticipated rout of Afghan forces, and the situation was relatively calm. We had full supplies and only two men were receiving treatment aboard our gondola. I had only recently been brevetted from Assistant Surgeon with the 5th Northumberland Fusiliers to Surgeon-Lieutenant for General Burrows' 66th Regiment of Foot. I was nervous, anxious, and a little excited at the prospect of watching the action from a high vantage point. Of course, it wasn't to be. The high crags and deep ravines of the mountain passes between Kandahar and Kabul were just as good for the Afghans to hide from us in the air as it was for them to ambush the men on the ground. The scouting ship ahead of us had missed them, and we were too low to avoid a surprise rocket attack against our flanks. We didn't even know they had rockets.

I burned that day, but not before we had steered the ship away from our attackers and beached ourselves upon the steep mountain slopes. As the ranking officer before we hit the ground, I had resolutely remained at my post while others fled; but the pain was damnable, and I had not the time to fight the overwhelming wave of darkness that took me even as the overhead balloons erupted into flame. I later learned that it was my loyal orderly, Murray, who returned to the gondola to rescue me. Carrying my unconscious body away from the explosion to safety behind a rocky outcrop, he would later assure me that it was only because I was the ranking officer. I knew otherwise, for Murray was a solid chap, and in saving me he allowed me to repay the debt by leading the survivors safely home. I hadn't seen him since. We were both mentioned in dispatches, but he returned to action while I had my feverish return to England to look forward to.

It had not occurred to me that the publication of these adventures within the pages of *The Strand* magazine might be a cause for reunion. I was pleasantly surprised when, one morning in early June, Holmes and I were interrupted by Mrs Hudson, who explained that a man had arrived to see me at the tradesmen's entrance.

"It is a rare occasion for a client to arrive by the back door," said Holmes after the landlady disappeared to bring our visitor upstairs.

"Hardly a client if he is here to see me, Holmes," said I. "A patient perhaps?"

"I think not, for Mrs Hudson has a wise head, and although she did not announce our guest's purpose, she would have introduced him as a patient if that were the case; and were you his debtor she would have sent him on his way."

I bridled a little at the suggestion that any visitor of mine would be seeking payment, but any further comment was postponed by a gentle tap upon our door.

"Come!" Holmes called, maintaining a languid and unconcerned repose as the door opened slightly and a familiar face peered through.

"My goodness! It's Murray!" I ejaculated, overcome with pleasure to see again the face of the man to whom I owed my life.

"Doctor Watson?" He shuffled nervously into the room, nodding courteously to Holmes before closing the door behind him. "I do hope I'm not intruding, gentlemen."

"Not at all, Mr. Murray," said Holmes, springing from his chair and crossing the room in a single bound. "Any friend of Watson's is a friend of mine. Please take a seat, for I note you've had a long and stressful journey. How recently did you arrive from the Continent? I do hope the baggage car on the last leg of your journey wasn't too cramped."

I stood agape as Holmes encouraged him to sit in my old armchair and proceeded to pour a tumbler of whiskey before offering soda from the gasogene.

"How... how did you know that?" Murray asked, clearly as surprised as I by the suggestion.

"While your pallor is disguised by tanning, the shadows beneath your eyes indicate that you haven't slept for a day or more. You don't appear to have changed your clothes recently either. You wear an ill-fitting railwayman's coat, and while you have unpicked the badge there remains a snag of red and white thread that matches the colours of the London, Chatham and Dover Railway Company. The only journey of any distance that company operates is Saint-Omer to London

by way of the Gladstone Tunnel. Even third class tickets are expensive and the journey normally merits dressing for the occasion, yet what you wear beneath—the remnant of an army uniform—is dishevelled and quite dusty, suggesting to me that your journey was not as a passenger. Your tan, the shade of your trousers and the fact that your army boots are well-scuffed and have not been bulled for some time lead me to conclude that you have travelled an even greater distance."

"That's correct Mister 'olmes. I am lately returned from Istanbul. I made for England post-haste to seek your 'elp and advice through the good graces of Doctor Watson here."

"My dear Murray," said I, "you know I would do anything in my power to assist you. What on Earth has brought you to this?"

"What on Earth, indeed, doctor," said Murray, his hands trembling as he gulped down the whiskey and soda, "for I fear what I have come to see you about may not be of this Earth."

"Not of Earth?" Holmes leaned forward, his interest piqued. "I have little interest in spiritual matters Mr. Murray, so I do hope that you're mistaken. I would be grateful if you could explain how you came to be here. Be sure not to omit the slightest of details."

"Very well, sir. As Dr. Watson knows, I stayed behind to see me service through after Maiwand and Kand'har, after which I joined the New East Indias, and I've been with 'em ever since. We mostly police the trade routes an' guard cargo between Bombay an' Istanbul. I'm mostly called upon to deal with heatstroke an' the odd death on the line. I've been banking me money and livin' on rations for the most part, an' I was lookin' forward to staying on 'til I got meself an out-pension."

"It all changed about a week back, when I 'ad orders to babysit a unit transfer. There's a unit—the grey company we calls 'em—they set aside for special duties. First thing that struck me when they turned up was that they never said a word; didn't act like normal blokes neither. Over an 'undred of 'em were packed into two carriages like pickles in a jar, marching in two by two with the blankest faces I ever saw. And the smell..."

"The smell?"

"Lavender oil. Very thick with it, they was. Not what you expect to smell on a man, let alone a soldier; but that wasn't all. They were strapped up with the weirdest bits of kit. Padded armour an' equipment I reckoned, but not worn like normal army webbin'. They 'ad thick boots an' elbow pads an' shoulder pads,

even what looked like neck braces; and no two were kitted out the same. It reminded me of a line o' wounded men walking back from battle, except that they was all stood up straight an' disciplined like new men ready to join a front line. I've never seen the like."

"What do you think, Watson?"

"I don't know Holmes," said I, "I've not much knowledge of the New East Indias, not since the Raj took over."

"Yes, my father was with the old East Indias," said Holmes, "and I've never come across any mention of this grey company before. Do you know what their mission had been? Or where they were bound?"

"They were bound for 'ome, sir. Here in London." Murray withdrew a folded docket from inside his coat and handed it to Holmes, who turned his attentions to its study while Murray continued. "That's partly why I'm here. I was only supposed to stay with 'em til their carriage was transferred to another train at Istanbul, but I decided I just 'ad to follow."

"Why would you do this?" Holmes asked, curiously. "Such dereliction of duty would surely risk your career, if not your life?

"Some things are more important. You know that, Dr. Watson. It's what I saw when we shipped 'em aboard as

changed my mind about things. We took 'em on at the Victoria Terminus. There was a rumour going round that they'd been clearin' local villages to make way for an engineering project to the north."

"I'm sorry," said I, thinking I had misheard. "Clearing?"

"You know, kickin' out the locals and movin' 'em on so the land can be used. Rumour has it there's going to be an aeroport built to the north east o' the city."

I was minded of the highland clearances, and shuddered at the idea that such policies might again rear their head barely thirty years after the last Indian rebellion.

"This docket," said Holmes, "the wording suggests that the men themselves were cargo or, more specifically, 'military ordnance'. That's not how a soldier is usually treated or described."

"Indeed not sir," agreed Murray, "and that added to my unease; but the worst of it was that I recognised one o' the men from a few months prior. Studeley was 'is name. He were a common soldier, a bit wet behind the ears. The thing is, I was there when 'e died."

"Died?" I said. "What are you saying? That he died in transit?"

"No, doctor," he shook his head. "Three months before that. He'd slipped while movin' between

carriages as we crossed the Alfred Viaduct over the Towa river. He toppled from the train an' fell a great distance to the rocks below. I was with the recovery party that carried 'im back. He was barely alive, but 'is body was shattered. We got 'im into 'ospital, but he died of his injuries."

"So," Holmes interrupted, "you didn't see him die?"

"As good as sir. He was unconscious an' never recovered."

"But you weren't there?"

"No, sir."

"Then it is reasonable to assume, if you were not mistaken, that he must have recovered."

"Remotely possible sir, but that's not what they told me, and I know injuries. The lad shouldn't have been able to walk again let alone return to duty."

"Did you speak with him the next time you met?"

"As I said, sir, none of 'em spoke. I did try, but 'e never even made eye contact."

"And do you recall what combination of 'padding' he sported?"

"The works sir. Arms, legs, neck brace. To my mind its like 'e still had the injuries I saw on 'im the last time. That's when I decided to stay inside 'is carriage, but at close quarters the lavender oil was overwhelmin'; so I stole that docket and switched from train to train with 'em, finding

whatever empty spaces I could until we reached London. I reckoned I might see if Dr. Watson here might get you to investigate. It's not right Mister 'olmes. Not proper."

"Quite. It is a noble sentiment, Mr. Murray, and one that I share. Leave the docket with me, and I shall investigate the matter for myself."

Crossing to the mantle-piece, Holmes withdrew a wallet that sat, nestled between several tobacco pouches. Drawing out a pair of notes, he handed them to Murray. "Here is some money for your troubles. Take up lodging nearby and let Mrs Hudson know where you will be staying so that we may meet with you upon our return. You may yet have a career to salvage, and if so Watson and I shall render whatever assistance we can to make it so."

With that, he ushered Murray from the room, closing the door firmly before turning to me.

"Well, Watson, what should we make of this?"

"As you know Holmes, I trust Murray with my life. He's too sensible to be a drinking man, and a sounder and more loyal orderly I could never hope to have met. If he says he saw this, then I must take his word on it."

"Quite so, and this?"

He handed me the docket, which identified a cargo of one hundred and twelve men for delivery to a place called the Medical Ordnance Company in Southwark.

"I've never heard of medical ordnance, Holmes. You can't describe men as weapons."

"And yet when you give a man a gun, that is exactly what he becomes; but it is not the top of the docket I must draw your attention to, but the bottom."

I looked at the foot of the docket, and to the signature. It was not, as I had expected, signed off by an officer or a surgeon of the New East Indias, but by a doctor called Shaw on behalf of a private research institute in Abingdon.

"The Knox Institute? What's that?"

"What indeed," said Holmes, holding out an index card he had retrieved while I examined the docket. "The Knox Institute of Transcendent Anatomy, established by Dr. Robert Knox in 1857."

"*The* Robert Knox," I asked, "the resurrectionist?"

"It would seem so, and while his involvement with the Edinburgh burkers is a matter of note, I can't help thinking that there is a connection."

"You can't just dig up a dead man's reputation," said I, somewhat inelegantly.

Holmes raised a curious eyebrow at my last remark, amused by its implications.

"It is the phrase *transcendent anatomy* that is of interest to me, Watson. What does it mean, exactly?"

"It's certainly never come up in *The Lancet*. Sounds like quackery to me."

"Only a moment ago you were reluctant to impugn a dead man's reputation, and in the very next breath you accuse him of quackery. Surely the truth must lie somewhere in between."

"I'm sure you're right, Holmes. Just because it sounds a little off doesn't make it madness."

"Your military and medical connections are far better than mine, Watson. See what you can find out today, and tomorrow morning we shall depart for Abingdon."

# II. An Eventful Evening

It is difficult for a medical man in London to be taken seriously if he does not attend some professional club or society. While I retain membership of the Abernethians from my student days, it offers little more than an annual dinner and so, over the years I have made a point of guesting at Chandos House every couple of months just to maintain some contact with my fellow professionals. The prospect of parting with a significant amount of money to give me access to a private club (where the drinks were even more expensive) has, however, never appealed.

My first port of call was therefore the surgeon's bar at Saint Barts, where I met with our old friend Stamford. After catching up over a couple of drinks he introduced me to another doctor, Charles Colman, who had heard something of transcendent anatomy as a field of research when, at the Royal Medical and Chirurgical Society, he had heard the thing discussed. He agreed, in return for further drinks, to take me that evening as a guest, and to introduce me to the source of his recollection.

It was a quarter to nine when we arrived at Berners Street, whereupon we were ushered upstairs past the library, the dining room and some meeting rooms, into the lounge. Here Colman called for some cognac before introducing me to Dr. Joshua Pryce of King's College London. He was happy to discuss his understanding of transcendent anatomy with fellow surgeons, for this was the purpose of a professional society after all. Just so long as I kept him well topped up.

"Imagine," Pryce began, "a scientific method by which the human capacity can be improved. Where Francis Galton identified a possible link between ancestry and mental superiority, there have been others who believe that science might be used to make the mind and body more resilient by external means. Just as we use drugs and medical aids to provide relief or to heal, might they not also be used to make the legs faster or the bones stronger or the organs more efficient?"

"That's a reasonable avenue to explore," I agreed, "just so long as the side-effects don't jeopardise the long-term health of the patient. If it puts a man's short-term effectiveness ahead of his long term welfare, then it cannot be allowed."

"Quite, James; although the term patient suggests you are thinking of men with ailments, rather than those deemed fit for military service. In times of war, where the lives of men are bartered for territory and power, such considerations might not be so great."

"So that's what the Knox Institute is about?" I ventured.

Pryce nodded. "Knox poured all his wealth into a research institute in order to apply his expertise in anatomy to the improvement of the body through medicines and appliances. Sir William Fergusson took over when he died, and then Fergusson passed the baton to the current President, Sir Joseph Lister."

"Fergusson and Lister?" I repeated in some surprise. Pryce couldn't have come up with two bigger names in contemporary medicine if he tried.

"Fergusson was pretty hands-on, but for Lister it's mostly titular. A lot of the new electropathic equipment he trials at his new surgical unit comes from the Knox Institute."

I nodded. The aseptic surgery at King's College was reputed to be the best in all of Europe. If I could have my days as a medical student over again it would be my first choice to study. I resisted questioning Pryce any further for fear of showing too much interest, for it is never a good idea to question the reputation of a surgeon as great as Lister. I changed the topic to more pleasurable pursuits like golf and fly-fishing, making my excuses as the evening drew to a close and returning to Baker Street at the first opportunity.

***

It was close to midnight when I returned to our rooms, and the streets were quite deserted. In the distance I spied a faint glow and a thin pall of smoke to the south of the river—a warehouse or slum fire I presumed. The older parts of the city were overcrowded and in need of much rebuilding. As my cab pulled up outside our Baker Street rooms I could see Holmes' brilliantly lit silhouette as he paced back and forth, pausing only to acknowledge my arrival through the window.

With the hour being late Holmes came down to greet me, and, I am sure, to check my sobriety. It had been a long night for me, and I could already smell the spirit through my pores. Unusually, he sat me down and waited upon my own experiences before launching into an account of his own.

"Splendid work, Watson. I agree that, with Lister and Fergusson behind it, the Knox Institute has impeccable credentials. There is more to this matter than meets the eye, which is why I took a little excursion

down to the offices of the Medical Ordnance Company in Southwark for a spot of breaking and entering earlier this evening."

"You did what?" I was quite angry with Holmes, sending me off to get tipsy while he was risking his reputation on an undeniably criminal act.

"You should know by now Watson, that I do not do these things without careful consideration. I first disguised myself as a dragon-chaser out of limehouse. The heavy stink of opium smoke and my apparent lethargy would buy me the time I might needed to make my escape and to not be taken seriously if discovered. A precaution it was well for me to take."

"The Ordnance Company lies off the Jamaica Road not far past Shad Thames. A rough spot in the daytime, it looks even worse at night. I couldn't have got closer to the docks without being in Bermondsey itself, and I suspect the location was chosen precisely because of its easy access to the river. It has high walls and no accessible windows, with the only way in being a guarded arch. Fortunately, the south-facing wall is in a poor state of repair, and a tree brushed across the top at the midpoint between a pair of old gas street lamps not yet upgraded. Even better, the wood was sturdy enough for me to cast a rope over its bough and pulley myself up using a looped knot. From there I could see the bough continued some feet past the wall, over an enclosed courtyard."

"Balancing upon the wall, I counted three storeys altogether, with barred windows on the first two. The only way up to that level was a cast iron drainpipe, which I decided to risk. Dropping to the ground I produced the leather climbing strap we recovered from the Tudor Mansions case and tested the pipe against my weight. It was then a matter of a minute or two to pull myself up to the higher level, where a wide ledge allowed me to use my bradawl to attack the heavy sash mechanism with some vigour."

"I confess I was uncertain of what my evening's investigations might reveal, but every room presents a different opportunity. The top floor was clearly administrative, and I was able to view a number of patent records for devices trialled and tested by the Knox Institute and then manufactured by the ordnance company. Most of these apparati related to the manufacture of body braces, harnesses, clevis pins and armoured casings to protect the various electropathic stimulators or chemical injectors. There were miniaturized timing mechanisms, and all manner of

prostheses and implantations. All perfectly legitimate from a medical perspective, but quite suspicious in combination."

"Dissatisfied with mere paperwork, I descended lower, into what I assumed was the manufactory. The first floor was a high-ceilinged, open space, and yes, in the moonlight that flooded through the windows I could make out assembly tables and parts baskets, lasts and lathes and material swatches. All the things one might expect in a workshop producing medical harnesses. But there was more."

"The workshop was lined with the new incandescent bulbs, and I was able to fill the room with brilliant light as I flicked on a switch close to the door. Where there had been shadows I could now see that around a dozen cages lined the inner wall of the workshop. Each of these contained a strap-down tilt-table on which..."

"Yes, Holmes," I encouraged him, "what did you see?"

"They were men, Watson, strapped to the tables and sleeping like the dead. Beside each was a neat pile of clothes—their East India uniforms. They wore only undergarments beneath elasticated body braces, and each man was connected to a number of intravenous catheters. You would have made more of it than I, but to a layman's eye these tubes appeared to be drawing thick black blood out of their bodies, passing it through a spinning mechanism that distilled it into a bright red form, and then mixing it with fluid from another catheter before returning it back into their bodies."

"Filtering poisons from the blood I presume. Did you sample the additive?"

"I did," said he, drawing a small brown bottle from his pocket. He passed the drug to me and I unscrewed the lid, withdrawing the small glass pipette. I sniffed the concoction. It was a saline tincture that included morphine, aconite and something akin to celery or fennel.

"A potent anaesthetic," I concluded, urging Holmes to continue.

"Fortunately for me. I suspect the poisons being filtered were created by infections."

"Why do you say that, Holmes?"

"Each man appeared to have various body parts tied off to eliminate the flow of blood. As Murray had observed, there was an overwhelming smell of lavender oil, but beneath it I could smell the rot. Arms and legs were isolated by metal pins inserted through flesh and bone, then capped with rubber seals liberally applied with alcohol and iodine as if to stave off the spread of their infection."

"That's appalling, Holmes. Surely the army cannot be complicit in that?"

"Not the army, Watson, but the New East India Company. I am not a religious man, but the application of the science of transcendent anatomy can only be described as unholy."

"Indeed," said I, as shocked as my companion. I thought back to Pryce's description of the work, and shuddered at the thought of someone doing this in a time of relative peace. "What happened next?"

"I made an error of judgement, Watson. One so terrible that I will be forced to live with the consequences until my final breath. The cages, you see, were only locked from the inside, and I was desperate to make a further inspection. Opening the nearest, I stepped inside and examined the man that lay there more closely."

"There were no personal effects or papers identifying him, but there was, tied to his neck with butcher's twine, a Prussian *hundemark*."

"A what?"

"A dog tag. Used on the streets of Berlin to mark the ownership of dogs, the Prussian army adopted them as a means of identifying the injured and the dead during the Franco-Prussian War. Several armies have considered using them, and I must assume the New East Indias have adopted the practice. This one was round and made of soft brown metal, into which some basic information—the letters NEIC followed by name, rank, service number and a date—had been crudely impressed. His name was Ashleigh, and he had been a Corporal. The date intrigued me—04-08-79—not a date of birth, for he would be only five years old, so what? The date he joined the grey company, perhaps?"

"Up close I withdrew my pocket knife and cut away his vest to examine him in more detail. He was hairless, and his chest was marred by multiple scars which, from their length and the quality of the stitches, must have been medical in nature."

"Finally, and most foolishly, I withdrew the catheters, holding back the last—the one pushing bright red blood into his veins—until the very last moment. Optimistically I had brought a small vial of smelling salts with me, which I applied before standing well back, for I desperately wanted to speak with the man. At first there was no reaction, so I waited a few moments before applying the salts again, and this time he reacted. It was a deep, guttural moan, soon followed by the flickering of his eyelids and the clarity of consciousness within his pupils. He stared at me, Watson, his bloodshot eyes conveyed not just the depth of his pain, but also the anger

and distress that his condition had instilled upon him. Within moments he was straining hard against the leather straps of the tilt-table, and I considered, very briefly, releasing him from his bondage. There was, however, no need, for the straining of his muscles against the leather soon caused it to snap. I stood there, my voice hoarse, questions racing through my mind. His eyes fixed upon me as I stepped back, out of the cage. The pupils were wide, and there was no sign of any muscular activity in the face, which remained impassive even as the body strained to unleash itself."

"Uncertain of what to expect, I tried to reason with Corporal Ashleigh; to calm him down. Eventually, detached from the tilt-table, he took a step towards me and spoke at last."

"'Halt,'" he said "'Identify yourself!'"

"Naturally, I backed away as he stretched his hands out towards me, but I found my retreat blocked by worktables. I delivered a flurry of neat blows to his nose, jaw and abdomen, but it was like punching a side of beef. He easily swatted my fists aside before his hands quickly and precisely found my windpipe. I have never been in greater fear for my life than at that moment, when the image of my death at the hands of some inhuman beast flashed before my eyes. I was leaning so far backwards that I feared my spine might give before I lost consciousness, while this... creature that so resembled Mary Shelley's creation bore down upon me."

"I desperately scrabbled for a makeshift weapon on the worktable behind me. Even as pins and needles closed around my head I could feel the haft of something loose within my grasp. Swinging it around with all the force that I could muster, I found myself plunging a screwdriver deep into the side of my attacker's head, perforating the eardrum and driving it directly into the left hand side of his brain."

"The Corporal's fingers opened involuntarily and I gasped for breath. A moment later I saw a trickle of blood emerge from one of his nostrils. I jiggled my makeshift weapon as he pressed upon me again, sliding myself from beneath his heavy body as he crashed onto the work-top."

"Gasping for air, I resolved to brush up on my hand-to-hand skills, for my survival had been due more to chance than to preparation. Even then, with his brains scrambled, the Corporal lurched up with a manic glint in his eye, and reached again for me. I placed my foot squarely onto his midsection and pushed, tipping him to the floor where, again, he began to stir. A glance to the worktable revealed an toolbox, which I took a hold of, heaving it solidly above my

head before using all my remaining strength to hurl it directly onto his head."

"Good grief, Holmes," I said at last, having found myself wince at the graphic nature of my friend's account. As a doctor I had seen and heard a great many things, but this was unlike any I had heard, and to see fear in Holmes' recollections was a new experience for me, for nothing had shaken him as deeply as this encounter with the lavender men.

"What happened next? The others—"

"So help me, Watson, I made sure that he was dead, and then I gathered up the *hundemarken* from the others while they slept and then... I killed them. I killed them all. I smashed the fluid bottles and spread alcohol across the workshop. I ignited a match and then retreated to the top floor where I set fire to all the records I had found there before making my escape. Even as we speak the factory burns."

# III. Ashes to Ashes

Spread across the dining table of our Baker Street apartment were the scattered identification tags of those that Holmes had killed, and I could not help but think about the men that had worn them. Soldiers with families, all snuffed out in the most grotesque circumstances. While I struggle to condone Holmes' actions, I do so in the knowledge that he had no choice, and that these men's bodies had been so abused that they were already *as good as dead.*

We abandoned our plans to visit Abingdon that morning, having both spent a sleepless night considering the consequences of the night's events. When it arrived *The Times* carried some sensationalist news of the blaze, but made no mention of the men that had died.

It was Holmes that eventually broke the silence with a considered view of what might happen next. At the time I was still overcome with a combined sense of shock and gratitude, relieved that I had not been a party to these men's demise.

"We will receive a visitor soon," said Holmes, "and the identity of that visitor will determine what happens next."

"How so?" I asked, uncertain of Holmes' logic in the matter.

"If the police arrive, it will just be to seek our assistance in the matter. If it is my brother, Mycroft, then I must conclude that the government is indeed complicit in these events."

"Then we must hope it is the police."

"Indeed, for if our visitor is an agent of those we are investigating, then we are to be silenced, and your friend Murray may already be dead."

***

Within the hour our visitor had arrived by hansom and stood at the centre of our apartment where Holmes stood with his back to the door, staring out of the bow window and out onto Baker Street. He was a tall and quite distinguished man in his late thirties, just over six feet tall with a broad ginger moustache that met a full set of sideburns. His green bowler matched his checkered suit, which succeeded in drawing attention away from the young constable that accompanied him.

"Inspector Garrett of M Division," said Holmes before the officer could introduce himself. "I see from the traces of soot around your forearms and on your shoes that you've had

a busy morning sifting through the ashes of a recent fire. The same blaze that Watson and I could see from across the river during the early hours."

"Indeed, Mr Holmes," said Garrett, clearly impressed by the observations. "The Medical Ordnance Company of Southwark was broken into and burned to the ground last night, and I would be grateful if you would oblige me with your assistance in the matter."

"What assistance is it that you require, inspector?" Holmes said with a familiar, if fabricated, air of impatience. "What is the mystery that you wish unravelled?"

"Well, the identity of the arsonist is our goal. We do have a suspect, but his description does not match that of the man whose burned body we recovered from the fire."

"There was a body? The arsonist self-immolated?"

"So it would appear," said Garrett. "The night watchmen are accounted for and the building was secure, and yet the fire was started from deep inside, close to where a body was found."

"If you have your culprit, and nobody is in immediate danger, why are you so quick to involve me in the case?"

"I have a feeling, Mr Holmes. There was an hours delay between the departure of the Metropolitan Fire Brigade from the scene and the involvement of Scotland Yard. Someone high up kept us back, and when I arrived it was clear to me that the evidence had been tampered with."

"In what way?"

"Several large objects were removed from the premises after the fire. The ash had been moved and trampled on by the firemen, but it was plain to my trained eye that something was amiss."

"Then you have your man, inspector," said Holmes, reaching for an overcoat, "your carriage awaits!"

***

The fire on Jamaica road had been contained by the surrounding courtyard, which Holmes took time to examine before returning to join us at the front of the building. The exterior had survived, but it was little more than a blackened husk. The top two stories had collapsed onto the ground floor, where the remains of the body had been found. It was difficult to circumnavigate the building's shell, but Holmes picked his way through the debris, calling out questions of the inspector as he disappeared between charred beams and behind scorched brickwork.

"So, inspector, what exactly is the

medical ordnance that this factory produced?"

"Prosthetics and orthopaedic harnesses, so I understand. There's certainly no sign of weaponry, and there's no licence for munitions."

"Not exactly ordnance, then," said Holmes. "Unless the prosthetics have concealed guns and the harnesses are for flame-throwers."

"I wondered that myself," the inspector smiled, "but I suppose having exclusive contracts with the military they felt the name was appropriate."

"Oh?" Holmes paused, pointing out the black marks in the ground that had led Garrett to conclude that something large and heavy had been dragged from the debris and loaded onto a carriage of some kind. Doubtless these had been the cages and the tilt-tables Holmes had described, each of which would have contained a charred corpse much like the body that had been dug from the rubble. "I thought the military preferred a high degree of precision among its contractors? That would suggest that they must also supply medical weapons. Perhaps biological or chemical agents, or devices to improve military effectiveness."

"Perhaps," said the inspector. "The Fire Brigade have been little help, and the night-watchmen are even more tight-lipped. Mr Riordan, the general manager, is arriving with an insurance agent within the hour."

"The Brigade is in the pay of the insurance companies, is it not?"

"My thoughts exactly, Mr. Holmes. For some reason this fire needs to be an accident, even for the insurers."

I could see that Holmes was enjoying his conversation with Garrett. Lacking the competitive edge shared by his colleagues north of the river, the inspector seemed more interested in rooting out the cause of the crime than bulldozing his way through the investigation. Holmes, meanwhile, disappeared for a moment, examining the place where his attacker—the alleged arsonist—had come to grief.

"So, inspector, where does this suspect of yours come from if you've not got anything useful from the witnesses?"

"A 'gram was received two days ago telling us to be on the look out for a medical orderly from the New East Indias. He went absent from his post about a week earlier while travelling from Bombay with a cargo bound for this very factory. According to the Ordnance Company the delivery turned up but the orderly had vanished."

"I see. And what was the cargo?" Holmes asked.

"Classified, so I am told," said

Garrett, clearly unimpressed. "I assume that it was supplies but we're awaiting confirmation."

"Supplies? There is the a storage facility then? Holmes asked.

"We only hold working stock on the premises," came a new voice, interrupting the exchange between the two detectives. The newcomer was a short balding man with thick eyebrows and heavy-lensed spectacles. He offered his hand out, first to Garrett and then to Holmes. "My name is George Riordan, and I'm the General Manager. This—" he indicated a tall thin man stood slightly behind him "—is the insurance agent, Mr. Kaettler."

"Do carry on gentlemen," the tall man said in a faintly continental accent, touching the brim of his hat before turning to survey the scene for himself, "and do not mind me, I would like to conduct my investigation separately."

"One moment," said Holmes, offering his hand; "as we are in similar professions, perhaps we might we exchange trade cards?"

It was a rare request from Holmes, and Kaettler responded instead with a short bow before the cards were duly shared. Glancing briefly at it, my friend allowed Kaettler to excuse himself and resume his investigations.

"Mr Riordan, was your East Indiasman a Corporal called Ashleigh?"

"Ashleigh?" Riordan repeated the name slowly, "why, no. His name is Murray. I don't know of any Ashleigh."

"Odd," said Holmes, producing one of the dog-tags he had acquired the night before. It was covered in soot, as were his fingertips. "I found this tag in the rubble where your arsonist's body was discovered. It bears the name of a Corporal Ashleigh, and the letters NEIC which, I presume, denote the New East India Company."

"So, our arsonist isn't Murray after all," said Garrett, pulling out a pocketbook and making a short note.

"No, no, that's not possible," said Riordan testily.

"Why not? This is an East India dog tag is it not?" Holmes held out the *hundemark*, which Riordan took from him to examine.

"It is," Riordan agreed at last, "but we have East Indias here all the time. The Company is one of our biggest customers. It could have been anybody's."

"Anyone who happened to drop it in the exact same spot where a suspected arsonist fell? Indeed, Mr Riordan."

"May I see that," asked Kaettler, stepping forward to pluck the dog

tag from Riordan's fingers and inspect it for himself. "Mr Holmes has a point I'm afraid. But a crime needs a motive. What possible motive could this Ashleigh fellow or the other one have for burning down a factory?"

"The entire crime is motiveless so far as I can see," suggested Riordan.

"On the contrary," said Holmes, "if the suspect is a military man and the target of the arson is a supplier of military supplies then there *must* be a motive. Now that you are here, Mr Riordan, perhaps you can tell us about the ordnance you made here."

"I cannot. Our products are far too complex for me to describe to a non-medical man."

I coughed at this, and Holmes smiled, drawing me into the conversation.

"This is my companion, Dr. Watson, both a medical man and a former army surgeon. If you cannot explain to him, then I fear nobody will understand."

Riordan flushed, and stumbled over his hasty explanation. "We use the term ordnance quite loosely. The harnesses and braces we make here are designed to help a man get back to the front line as quickly as possible, feeding him the pain relief and physical support he needs to stay at his post in spite of his injuries."

"Really?" said I, unconvinced. "No doctor would accept such a responsibility. It breaks our sacred oath to do the best for our patient. I could not in good conscience allow an injured man to stand and fight when his life might be in danger. I need to see these harnesses and to better understand how a doctor might prescribe their use in the theatre of war."

"Precisely," smiled Holmes, clapping a hand upon my shoulder and addressing Inspector Garrett. "I believe we need to meet with the researchers responsible for developing the equipment that was stored here. If there was some kind of malfunction that caused injury or death to a soldier in service, then that might provide the motive you seek."

"Indeed it might, Mr Holmes," said Garrett, as he rounded upon the businessman. "Where are these items designed and tested, Mr Riordan?"

"I cannot say," the businessman protested. "That information is classified."

"Poppycock," I ejaculated. "It's common knowledge in medical circles that these devices are developed by the Knox Institute."

"It is?" Riordan's face fell as Garrett and Kaettler turned on him, taking notes and pushing for more

information while Holmes stepped back and took me by the arm.

"Sterling work, Watson," he whispered. "I do believe you've given us a legitimate excuse to take our enquiries north."

# IV. The March of the Grey Company

Returning to Baker Street, Holmes was keen to make progress with the case. Hastily transcribing the information from the *hundemarken*, he despatched me to the park end of the Foreign and Commonwealth Office at St. James' while setting off on an errand of his own. Although the New East Indias had kept a standing army, all military records were retained and publicly accessible at the India Office. With help from one of the clerks it took me less than an hour to confirm that the dozen bodies Holmes had discovered had been reported as killed in colonial service.

We met again at four in the afternoon on the platform of Paddington Station, where Inspector Garrett was more than happy to let Holmes and myself accompany him to Abingdon, where he was due to meet with the Director, Dr. Charles Street, at six.

"Something's not right with this case, Mr Holmes," said Garrett. "First I get a 'gram waiting at the station telling me to pull you from the case, and then some tramp delivers a bag of sooty dog-tags just like the one you found and a docket describing the cargo being transported to the Ordnance Company as *a hundred and twelve men*.

"Really?" I asked, glancing at Holmes, whose eyebrows were raised in mock surprise and innocence.

"Indeed, Dr. Watson, and I have my suspicions that at least a dozen of those men were involved with the fire, for I recovered twelve dog tags. That leaves a hundred more unaccounted for."

"A hundred?" Said Holmes. "It seems our East India contingent is growing by the hour. But if they were cargo—"

"—they might not have been alive?"

"Precisely, inspector," Holmes smiled. "I suggest you check the names you have with the East India records. It could well be that these men were being delivered in coffins."

"Good thinking! That would explain what was removed from the scene. I'll have the Company records checked when we get back, Mr Holmes."

"Splendid idea. It seems clear to me that your investigation is falling into place. Might I enquire as why you continue to retain my services, especially if my involvement goes unappreciated?"

"I don't like being bullied, Mr. Holmes, and I dislike cover-ups even more. Just because some bureaucrat in Whitehall snaps his fingers doesn't mean I have to dance to his tune."

"Very well then," said Holmes, "but might I suggest we separate when we get to our destination? If the powers that be don't want me involved, the least we can do is conceal the fact. And if I do get found out my continued involvement can come as a complete surprise to you."

"That seems a sensible approach," said Garrett, who, despite being duped by Holmes and myself, had the makings of a very fine detective. "Are then any questions you might like me to ask on your behalf?"

Holmes smiled, and reaching into his pocket produced a folded sheet of paper.

***

We planned to part at the station, and as we alighted I spotted a familiar face disembarking further down the platform.

"It's Kaettler, the insurance agent."

Garrett raised his hand to draw the fellow's attention, but Holmes intervened, gripping his wrist and lowering it.

"Inspector, remember your suspicion of an insurance set up? If Kaettler is on the same business as you then your paths will surely cross

at the Institute. If not, then it might be more prudent that Watson and I investigate from a safe distance."

Accepting Holmes' logic, we kept our distance and three separate carriages departed Abingdon station. While Garrett and Kaettler's carriages took the most direct route, Holmes and I took a more surreptitious approach, hanging back until we saw Kaettler's carriage peel away and take a side lane. Maintaining a discrete distance, our coachman let us off beside a wooden copse just shy of the brick wall that lined the rear of the estate.

We saw Kaettler's coach pass through a small arch and into a cobbled courtyard surrounded by a cluster of outbuildings several hundred yards from the main Institute.

"Interesting," said Holmes, "and not what I was expecting."

Picking our way through the woods, we reached the edge of the estate where a short fence separated us from the courtyard and Kaettler's carriage. The buildings looked like a small farmstead with a separate house, a barn and a long stable, but with no animals present or any sign of the mess one might expect of a working farm. Stepping over the fence we cautiously entered the yard, obscured from the main house by the barn wall.

"You see the front door, Watson? Black paint and brass trim. Very businesslike. These buildings must be a converted annex to the main hall, and doubtless Mr. Kaettler's place of work."

"Why would an insurance—"

"Kaettler is no more an insurance agent than you. His trade card identified him as a Paddington," he used the term dismissively, "and while insurance work can fall within such a remit, he made no practical examination of the fire scene and made no attempt to exchange details with Inspector Garrett or to ask us to report what we had found. I must conclude he has been retained as a private security agent."

While claiming to be London's 'premier private inquiry agency', the Paddingtons or *paddies* were often derided as the 'poor man's Pinkertons' ever since their founder, Ignatius Paul Pollaki, had retired. The company had originally been set up to root out Confederate spies in London during the war in America, but quickly fell into hiring police veterans from mainland Europe to offer the sort of private inquiry and security service that lacked Holmes' moral compass. On occasion I had heard him chide the crudeness of their advertising or the respectability of their clients. He had conducted one or two remedial investigations for clients dissatisfied with the Paddingtons' services, but as a rule if a client had approached them first Holmes was unlikely to be interested in taking the case.

"If the Knox Institute carries out research for military or other government purposes, then there must be someone in the field to protect their interests, and as a private concern the Institute requires private security. Kaettler, I suspect, is the man who exposed my involvement in the case, either out of professional jealousy or else fear that I might intervene."

Checking that we were unobserved from any window facing the courtyard, Holmes and I slipped into the barn from where we might get a better view of the house and stables. As with any barn, it was stacked high with bales of dried hay. There was a wooden stair up to the hayloft, which Holmes and I ascended stealthily, but with some speed.

"Wait!" Holmes stayed me halfway up the stair. "Do you smell that?"

I sniffed the air.

"Cooked meat?" I ventured.

"Indeed, Watson," said he, pointing down into the centre of the barn, "human meat."

I followed his gesture to see several empty cages, charred with soot, stacked against a wall of hay bales. Beside them, piled in a heap, was a

tangled mass of charred tilt-tables, each still carrying the scorched remains of a human being.

My gorge rose, and I turned to descend the stair, but Holmes placed a hand upon my shoulder.

"We know enough about them, Watson, and there is nothing we can do. Follow me."

***

The Hayloft provided an excellent vantage point for Holmes and I to use his binoculars to view the outbuildings, the Institute and the estate. The grounds were well-tended, but showed little sign of use, while there was a fair deal of activity in the immediate vicinity of the main hall. The carriage used by Garrett had departed, and a black, motorized coach was being readied for a journey. Resting on the ground to the right of the institute was a tethered aerostat that bore the livery of the Medical Ordnance Company. Closer to us Holmes scrutinized that part of the farmhouse facing us, whose interior décor confirmed its use as an office annex of some kind. In the courtyard below there was a steam-tug. Used to load and unload cargo from aerostats, and to tow cargo 'stats to and from their embarkation points along the national transport network, this particular tug had—if Holmes' interpretation of the black smudges on the attached trailer was correct—been used to ferry the cages from the airship to the barn.

"I want to have a look at the long stable, Watson," he said after some minutes of observation. "The use of modern vehicles and the absence of any owned coaches suggests to me that horses may not be in great demand here, and the separation of the Institute from its security suggests some prudence in keeping its secrets away from casual visitors."

Returning to the barn entrance, we were but twenty feet from the stables that lay across the cobbles. From there I could see that its doors were all bolted and padlocked, a fact that Holmes was already prepared for, having withdrawn a small leather roll-up filled with picks and skeleton keys. Drawing two items—one pick and an 'L' shaped bar—Holmes was across the yard and working upon the main lock in a matter of seconds, while I looked towards the farmhouse where, thankfully, I saw no sign of activity. With the door open Holmes looked out into the yard before—satisfied we were still unobserved—he beckoned for me to join him.

I marched across the cobbles as if taking a Sunday constitutional, straight through the stable door which Holmes closed behind me. The smell that hit me as I crossed the

threshold was the quite overpowering smell of lavender oil with a note of camphor wax. The room beyond shocked me to my core, for it was a brutal mockery of the very best aseptic morgue that medicine might afford. The stables had themselves been cut away and the doors walled over, so the space inside could best be described as a thoroughly scrubbed white-tiled chamber filled with a combination of medical apparatus and butcher's tools. A row of heavy ceramic tables ran along the length of the room—I counted twenty—each of which was occupied by a human body. On the opposite side of the stables was a row of doors with hatches that wouldn't have looked amiss in a modern gaol.

While I moved to the nearest body to conduct a visual examination, Holmes was at the nearest cell door, slipping back the hatch and peering inside.

"Eight," said Holmes, glancing toward me, "and still alive."

Eight men to a cell, ten cells and twenty on the tables. We had found the grey company, and it had been far easier than I had expected, and far more harrowing. What lay before us was the greatest nightmare a man sworn to uphold the Hippocratic oath might face. The abuse of medical knowledge and techniques with no consideration for ethical practices.

*They* were the medical ordnance in which the company traded, with a greater disregard for the human condition than even the old slaver-masters of the southern states.

The body on the bench nearest to me was pale, cold, and riddled with a mixture of scar layers and metal implants. Iron hoops were being used as permanent tourniquets on three of the four limbs. Each of these was screwed heavily into position by wing-nuts, and the flesh beyond the cut-off points was clearly necrotic. Drawing a pen from my pocket I carefully prodded the rotten flesh, only to find a steely resistance that was more like calcified bone than putrescent skin. All across the torso I could see open, bloodless wounds that had puckered around row upon row of needle tracks.

"This is obscene, Holmes," I said at last, drawing my handkerchief to my face. "This man has multiple fractures that have gone unhealed, and the implanted pins are beyond counting. It's as if he was fixed by an engineer, not a doctor."

"They are all like it, Watson. The bastard sons of medicine and mechanics, waiting to be fixed up, given fresh blood and returned to their duties in the East. We should end this, and swiftly."

"Like you did last night?" I turned on my companion. "I cannot. These

men must be saved, treated or given some humane means to end their suffering. While I cannot condemn your actions, Holmes, neither can I fully condone them. You at least are not protected by an oath, but you must surely see that our duty here is to these men and not to their destruction."

Holmes eyed me with a steely look. His jaw clenched as he considered my words and the consequences of any quarrel between us on the matter.

"Very well," said he, drawing back the bolt that secured the cell he had been examining. "Let them be free!"

Passing along the cells he drew back bolt after bolt, opening the doors to free the men that lay beyond. Swiftly then, he joined me near the door, and ushered me outside.

"You have your revolver?"

"Indeed," said I, patting my pocket. "What have you in mind?"

"Direct action, my friend," he said, crossing the cobbles to the black farmhouse door, on which he rapped repeatedly with the head of his cane. Within moments the door was opened by a middle-aged man dressed as a medical orderly.

"Good day to you sir," my friend began. "My name is Sherlock Holmes and my associate here is Doctor Watson. Could you oblige me by informing Mr. Kaettler that we are calling on him?"

We were led up to the first floor, where the landing had been turned into a small reception area. I started to take a seat while the orderly disappeared into an adjoining office, but Holmes stopped me.

"One doesn't enforce a confrontation by waiting, Watson," said he, stopping the door from closing as he pursued the orderly in to the room.

"Excuse me! You can't just—

"It's alright, Willoughby," I heard Kaettler say as I followed Holmes inside. The Paddington was standing over a cradle-like device set into moulded shellac. In his hand he held what I quickly recognised as one of the new teslaphone receivers. "Good evening, Mr Holmes; Doctor Watson. It is a little late for house calls don't you think?"

"Mr. Kaettler," Holmes nodded. "Rather odd for an insurance agent to be installed on his client's premises. Would you care to explain your deception at Southwark to myself and the good doctor?"

Kaettler smiled, dismissing Willoughby and gesturing for us both to take a seat. This time we complied, although I was careful to keep my hand close to my concealed revolver in case of any trouble.

"You are in deeper than you can possibly know, Mr. Holmes. This is a matter of the strictest confidence,

and one that involves the security of the Empire. You should leave such matters in the hands of professional detectives. You are merely an amateur..."

"I can assure you, Gustav," said Holmes, causing both Kaettler and myself to raise our eyebrows at his use of the Paddington's first name, "that I am more familiar with the secrets of the British Empire than either you or your *foreign volunteers* could ever hope to uncover, and my methods aren't learned from a lecture by a gifted dilettante like Ignatius Pollack, nor from your previous career as a second rate clerk working for the Prussian State Police. They have been honed by years of research and practical observation."

Kaettler replaced the receiver, smiling coldly as he stepped from behind his desk.

"I can assure you, gentlemen, that research and observation are just two of the tools in my arsenal. I was not a clerk as my records might show, but an agent of the state. Had I been a supporter of Bismark I would have risen to a senior position, but instead I came here, to England, where my skills can be put to better use in a private capacity. Here, you are on private property, where you have not only trespassed, but forced yourself into my office."

"I'm prepared to take my chances,

Kaettler," Holmes replied. "Your employers might be preparing to make a pitch to Her Majesty's government, but they've been using East Indiamen for their tests, and the East India Company has not been accountable to the Crown since '58."

With blinding speed, Kaettler launched himself at Holmes, knocking my friend sideways with a blow aimed at the kidneys. Without pausing he took a swing in my direction, catching me a glancing blow as I ducked backwards. The blow was more solid than I expected, and in my dazed state I saw that he had struck me with a truncheon. As I crashed against the wall I was vaguely aware of Holmes stepping between us, having successfully rolled with the Prussian's blow, striking out at our attacker with his walking cane. The heavy truncheon blocked it, and there followed a flurry of swipes and parries as the two men danced around the room, displacing furniture as they vied for the upper hand.

Regaining my own composure, I picked myself up, reaching into my pocket and drawing out my service revolver. As I did so I heard a commotion to my right, coming from outside. The orderly, Willoughby, was retreating up the stair towards us, screaming something about an attack. I could see him stumble backward as one of the lavender

men appeared, lumbering over him like a walking corpse. Kicking and screaming, he struggled to defend himself as a pair of steely, necrotic fingers closed upon him and started to squeeze his skull.

"Holmes!" I shouted, launching myself into the reception area where I could better see the stairs to aim my service revolver. I fired twice into the lumbering soldier, catching him once in the shoulder and once in the chest. With barely a grunt, he completed his grisly task, crushing poor Willoughby to death before turning his dark eyes upon me. I fired two more rounds into the creature before backing into Kaettler's office once more. I slammed the door shut, grateful to find a brass key in the lock. Turning it, I returned my attention to the conflict between Holmes and Kaettler, but it was done.

Holmes, his hair in disarray, had his back to me, leaning out of the wide sash window though which his quarry had escaped. Joining Holmes, I looked to the cobbled courtyard below, where Kaettler fled towards the Institute.

Behind us there was a solid thumping against the office door. My friend and I turned to see it rattle with the blows. Together we cleared Kaettler's desk, sliding it against the locked door as a barricade, while Holmes turned his attentions to the teslaphone.

# V. The Iron Giant

Our escape from the lavender men was a close one. Following Kaettler's lead, we jumped down from the first floor office onto the cobbles below, where we could see the creatures—for they could no longer be called men—turning over the outbuildings in search of prey.

"Come, Watson!" Holmes urged. "They cannot be helped right now. We must get to the Institute."

It was a short distance, but with a hundred shambling soldiers in our wake it seemed much longer. Their minds, like those of ancient Viking berserkers, seemed to be set upon the death of all that stood in their way. Ahead of us, Kaettler had reached the Institute, and Holmes beckoned me towards the opposite end of the building, where we might find the main entrance. My head was sore and throbbing with pain from the Prussian's cudgel and I was sure the flesh was broken, but I had to focus on escape.

Eventually, we reached the side of the building, where we paused for breath alongside the black steam-coach we had seen earlier in the day. As Holmes began to examine the vehicle, I realised what must be going through his mind, and shook my head.

"You cannot do this, Holmes. Whatever drugs have addled their brains, and whatever chemicals pollute them, they are living, breathing human beings."

"Of course, Watson," Holmes agreed, "but the reality is that whichever hand it might be, they will be condemned."

Walking round to the front of the Institute, we stepped inside. We were confronted by a large atrium set before a set of double doors. These were framed by a pair of grand staircases that led up to a first floor balcony where a bearded gentleman with glasses, with Kaettler by his side, was addressing the staff —a combination of doctors, orderlies and officials—who filled the space before us.

"...small arms are to be broken out," said the man. "Mr Kaettler will see to it that every man is issued with a weapon and ammunition. Now, hurry, for there is no time to lose..."

The crowd broke up while Kaettler took a moment to point us out to his superior. With a nod, the bearded

man descended a grand staircase and came straight towards us.

"You," he said accusingly, "have caused no end of trouble with your meddling. What gives you the right—"

"Common decency," said Holmes commandingly, "requires that you end your schemes right now, Dr. Street. No doubt you know who I am, and Mr. Kessler will have informed you of my purpose."

"No crime has been committed here," said Street, squaring up to my friend, "except for a matter of trespass and assault. I am sure the police—"

"The police?" Holmes smiled at such a threat. "I'm sure they would be interested to know where Inspector Garrett is right now, for I saw him arrive not half an hour ago, and no coachman has been here since. Would you care to take me to him."

"You'll be seeing Inspector Garrett soon enough, Mr. Holmes," said Street, clearly brimming with anger. "In the mean time I must ask you to leave the premises."

"You want me to step outside and place myself at the mercy of your experiments? Or do you want me out in the open where I can accidentally be picked off by a gunshot in the middle of a crisis? I think not, Street."

Holmes stepped forward so that he was nose to nose with the doctor, before shoving the top if his cane against the underside of the shorter man's beard until he was forced to stand on his toes.

"Where is Garrett?" He demanded with a degree of menace I had rarely seen.

"Very well," said the doctor, struggling to speak until Holmes released him, "this way."

Street scuttled back up the stairs as the sound of gunfire came from outside. Any authority he had shown earlier had been drained by my companion's anger as he brought us to a long whitewashed corridor that ran the length of the Institute. Open windows along the corridor had been propped open, and staff armed with rifles were taking pot-shots at anything that moved in the grounds.

Three doors along we came to a large metal door, heavily bolted from the outside. Slipping back the locks, Dr. Street pushed it open to reveal a sparse room with two occupants. The first, slumped forwards and tied to a chair, was Inspector Garrett, who had been beaten and disarmed. The second had its back to us, but there was no mistaking what it— he—must have been.

It was an armoured giant, decked in greaves, vambraces and other metal plates but held together by a series of pinion gears and pistons offering a high degree of powered mobility.

On the back was mounted an engine of some kind, while the head was covered by something resembling a Sadler diving helmet.

With a hiss, the iron giant turned to face us, and inside I saw a face I could never have mistaken for another.

"Murray!" I cried, stepping into the room to greet one of only two men in the whole world with whom I would trust my life. In response, his mechanically-assisted arm swung around, smashing me backwards into the wall, where I fell like a discarded rag-doll. My ears rang and my vision blurred as I tried, unsuccessfully, to shake away the pain and disorientation that ailed me. I could hear the dull echo of Holmes' voice, but not the words, for the combination of ametropia, vertigo, and tinnitus was overwhelming. Fighting against unconsciousness—for I had no desire to be incapacitated twice in one day—I propped myself up and fought hard to bring my revolver back into focus. The sound of conflict made it difficult to judge my position, and all I could make out was a large shadow that loomed overhead. Squinting, I finally managed to focus just enough to see Murray's battle-suit with an outstretched arm, the grip of whose mechanized gauntlet was tightening around the neck of my good friend Sherlock Holmes.

With the greatest of care I took aim, and squeezed the trigger as the darkness overwhelmed me once more.

# VI. Consequences

As a doctor, I have no great love for hospital beds, especially when I find myself waking up without anyone to explain the circumstances. Concussion made the hazy recollection of events come slowly, and left a dozen nagging questions to which I could not possibly have given an answer. That I had survived was all I knew, and the empty chair at my bedside created a mix of emotions that I dare not record here.

For myself the injuries were easy to identify. Concussion, contusions, severe bruising, a couple of sore ribs, a stiff neck and some superficial damage around the left eye. I had been lucky, but I wondered about my dear friend, Sherlock Holmes and my saviour, Arthur Murray. I wondered also, how Inspector Garrett had fared, and how great his own injuries had been after a beating at the hands of the monster Murray had become.

Letting out a groan of despair at the possibility of their demise, I was almost oblivious to the polite cough that came from my left hand side. Unable to glance sideways, I turned my whole body to see the man sitting on the bed to my left.

"Holmes!" I cried, overjoyed to see that my friend had also survived the ordeal. Not unscathed perhaps, but in a better condition than I. There was superficial bruising about his cheeks—I could still see the imprint of those great mechanized gauntlets—and he had been fitted with a neck brace. He looked as uncomfortable as I felt, but wore the familiar Baker Street dressing gown over his nightshirt. "You're alive!"

"Indeed I am, Watson, and for that, I am forever in your debt."

"You are? Tell me, what happened to Murray?"

"He too is in your debt. Your aim, even when incapacitated, is as reliable as ever."

"I didn't kill him?"

Holmes smiled. "Far from it, my friend. Whether blind luck or a calculated shot, your bullet shattered the control mechanism fitted to the rear of his mechanized armour. With a single bullet you incapacitated him without inflicting any damage on his person."

"I vaguely recall— where is he now?"

"Receiving the best of care at the hands of Sir Joseph Lister himself. He is keen to preserve his reputation

and is conducting a thorough review into the Institute's affairs."

"You're saying he was innocent?"

"Of any crime, yes, although how much he had been aware of remains uncertain. Needless to say that Dr. Street is in custody and has been referred to the General Medical Council to consider a charge of infamous conduct in a professional respect."

"What of Kaettler and Inspector Garrett?"

"The latter is in a better state than you or I; as for Kaettler, the Paddington contract has been terminated although no charges have been brought. While I suspect he was responsible for Murray's abduction there is no evidence, and poor Murray was unconscious from the time he was taken to the moment he woke up inside that... thing."

"I presume that enforced medication was used to induce his violent state."

"Unfortunately, when the army arrived to secure the estate, everything was taken. We can only speculate, and you know how averse I am to that."

"The army? I thought you called your brother."

"Ah, yes," said Holmes. "You expected him to make a personal appearance? We had no choice but to trust in Mycroft."

"The lavender men—they're dead, aren't they?"

Holmes stood, looked me in the eye, and left the ward.

# EPILOGUE –
## A Meeting with M

Inspector Thomas Garrett sat nervously beneath the painting of a man surrounded by dogs whilst sitting in a jar that graced the fireplace of the Strangers' Room in the Diogenes Club. When the army had arrived, he had been presented with a handwritten note on stationery embossed with the words *Rectum in factum, non ratio* and the address of the Diogenes Club. Garrett had had no inkling of their meaning, but the instructions were clear:

*"Deliver the personal journal of Dr. Robert Knox to me, in person.*

*Speak of this to no-one.*
*M."*

For all his protestations about Whitehall bureaucrats, *this* bureaucrat was a force to be reckoned with, and Garrett had no intention of disappointing him. Within minutes of arriving, a large, stout man entered the room, taking a seat across the room from him. At first he ignored the man, whom he dismissed as a guest that had arrived early for dinner. However, a casual glance in the man's direction caught the steely eyes that fixed the inspector with their deep set gaze. Then he knew.

Was this M?

Mycroft Holmes beckoned for Garrett to join him, and the inspector gathered up the bundle of books he had carefully wrapped in brown paper and crossed the room, placing the package into into his hands.

"That will be all, inspector," he said, dismissing Garrett with a wave of his hand. The policeman paused awkwardly, and then, with a brief nod, he left the room. In his wake, large hands with fat fingers tugged at the string, folding back the paper to expose the red leather volumes that rested within. Examining their spines, he selected the one embossed with the year 1857, and began to flip through the pages until he settled upon an entry that corresponded to his understanding of events, and began to read:

*"To die once is expected, but to die twice is something of a mixed blessing. To fall into the dark chasm and to see what lies beyond and then, bidden by the force of science, to return and live again must fill a man with dread, for he knows what fate awaits, or with disappointment, for he has seen salvation snatched away.*

For my part, death has not come calling, for I am its agent, both in despatch and in the art of revival. By profession I was, until recently, a pathological anatomist at Dr. Marsden's Free Cancer Hospital, but I will forever be remembered as the resurrection man, or the boy who buys the beef. That youthful indiscretion has followed me from Edinburgh to London, where I was for years rejected as a surgeon and forced into writing about my trade. In that time I was often approached by burkers in awe of my reputation and keen to provide a similar service to their predecessors, Burke and Hare, in whose actions I am still held to be complicit by much of society.

While in my youth the access to fresh cadavers gave me some competitive advantage over my peers, in later life my observations were slowly being surpassed, and only the extent of my personal experiences sustained my reputation well into my sixty-sixth year. I was surprised then, to be visited by a gentleman of the highest influence and of the greatest discretion, with an offer to revisit the most notorious chapter of my life, and to consider a role that some might say fitted me like a muslin shroud, hand-stitched to suit my last repose.

It was late in the evening of January the 30th, 1857 and I was still at my office, as had been a habit for many years since the loss of my sweet wife. I sat writing up the day's medical notes at my mahogany bureau, set beneath the bright light of a gas lamp. This new role, the observation and classification of tumours, the investigation of their causes and the opportunity to research and test new treatments, had quickly become an obsession, as if I had been given a second chance in my final years. I should have been oblivious to distraction were it not for the creaking of the floorboards beyond my surgery door, and the sympathetic groan it made while opening. I turned, and there in its frame stood a pair of gentlemen the likes of which I shall never forget.

The first was extremely tall and broad, of Nordic origin I was certain. His blond hair and sparkling blue eyes betrayed the magnificence of his Viking ancestry. He wore a plain suit and derby, which seemed incongruous on so fine a physical specimen. From the position of his hand upon the open door, it was clear to me that in spite of his evolutionary superiority, he was merely the manservant, or bodyguard, of his elder.

Cold, heavy-lidded eyes regarded me from beneath a protruding brow and a high-domed forehead that dominated the shorter man's body. This, I could tell, was a man of intellect and power, whose physical aspect had no need of overstatement. He stood, motionless, his stare fixed upon me like some ancient

lord looking over some unfortunate serf that crossed his path in the midst of a hunt for larger prey. He wore a long black coat over a dark suit, and in his gloved hands he gripped a top hat.

'Doctor Robert Knox, I presume?'

'Indeed, sir, and you are..?'

'M———,' he said, matter-of-factly. 'I have an interest in your work, and I wish to procure your services.'

'My services? I'm afraid, as you can see, sir, I am gainfully employed...'

'That is of no matter. I will speak with William Marsden and he will release you from your obligations.'

'For how long?' I asked, uncertain of just who, or how powerful, this M——— fellow really was. In my experience no man would be quite so commanding of his fellow men unless he had the means, and the confidence, the back it up.

'Indefinitely. I require your services as the founder and titular head of The Knox Institute of Transcendent Anatomy. In return you shall be provided with a generous emolument for the rest of your life.'

I was taken aback by the suggestion, even as I wrestled with the meaning of M———'s words. That I should be named as the head of an institution bearing my name, but whose purpose remained alien to me, seemed absurd.

'Transcendent? Of what?'

'I require a greater understanding of the human anatomy and, in particular, how well it can withstand the environmental extremes. I wish to understand how a man might best survive in arctic conditions, deep beneath the sea, high up in the air, or even on another world. I wish to find ways of improving any physical deficit that might impair his performance or his consciousness in such conditions. To transcend the human capacity and to embrace the superhuman.'

I stood agape. For a moment I feared I may be incapable of speech, but I was fortunate to recover myself and to respond to his suggestion.

'What of transcending mortality?' I asked. 'Do you also have an interest in cheating death.'

'That is a fantasy unbecoming a man of science, Dr. Knox. What we do not need to accept is that dying should be easy, nor that we cannot extend both the longevity and the reach of life beyond the terrestrial sphere. It is also possible to investigate the animation of necrotic tissues or the duplication of anatomical features by artificial means. These, sir, are the methods by which such goals can be achieved.'

'I couldn't have put it better myself,' I said at last. 'What you offer is the holy grail of scientific endeavours. But it comes at a price. What you propose cannot be achieved by studying cadavers, but by working with living specimens. The observation of organs and tissues as they perform their daily routines. Society is not ready for such a leap of faith.'

'Perhaps,' said he, 'but I can see that you are ready for it, doctor. I can ensure discretion and as many bodies—alive or dead—as you require to commence your work.'

'So this is why you turn to me to do this thing and not take credit for such a thing yourself? I am already tainted by my opinions, and too old to be a threat.'

'You understand me well, doctor. Your age is indeed a primary consideration. Dead men tell no tales, and the dividends your work can reap will come long after your demise. The other reason is, as you suspected, your well-known moral stance. I cannot abide dealing with men who have no concept of the bigger picture, and you are a man who truly understands the greater good in this matter. You are also a teacher, a man who can bestow the same principles upon his peers, and who can guide those still hungry for success to greater and faster success. Time is of the essence, doctor, and I have other matters to attend to. It is better that I remain in the shadows for now, so that the world may reap the benefits of our work in the years to come.'

It was a fine speech, and as I recall the words I see there must have been passion behind their construction, and yet in the delivery there was none. The lips moved like those of a snake, and the sentences came out in a steady and unwavering statement of fact. To be so dispassionate about such a subject made me shiver with apprehension. There was a greater goal at stake here. Were his plans so well drawn out that my new institution would be nothing but a tiny cog in a much bigger mechanism?

My new institution. There, I had thought it. My mind was already made up and my hand unconsciously extended.

'Then we have a deal,' I said.

'Good,' he said, lowering his gaze towards my proffered hand which hung, untouched, in mid-air. 'I will be in touch.'

With those words, he turned and was gone, his great manservant closing the door behind him and their footsteps fading across the wooden boards."

# THE INFANT TARTINI
## by Adem Rolfe

## I. Necessary Distractions

Any follower of the adventures of Sherlock Holmes would be bound to notice that most of my narratives rely upon the existence of a client whose circumstances arouse my friend's curiosity. While such cases are the norm, there are those rare instances in which our involvement is circumstantial, and whose successful resolution is, to coin a phrase, for the greater good.

So it was with 'The Infant Tartini', a case whose disparate elements could only have been coordinated by a mind of the first water, and while events preceded it, our case proper began in the suburbs of Chelsea during the early hours of a Summer morning in the year 1888.

As the sun rose to the east, a brougham pulled up beside a high brick wall in a well-sheltered service street. Its lone passenger disembarked, tipping the cabbie and adjusting his clothes, minimising the risk of his face being seen. For the moment at least, the street appeared to be deserted. As the carriage rattled away across the uneven cobbles, the man made his way to the end of the wall where the street joined up with the much busier thoroughfare of Commercial Road. Cautiously, the man paused, taking in the scene ahead. Ignoring the sellers and commuters, he settled his gaze upon a patrolling constable. Waiting until the officer was caught up in the hustle and bustle of the morning's traffic, the man shucked off his hat and coat, setting them aside before crossing over the street to where a large steam dray was being unloaded into a factory yard by a pair of powerfully built foreigners—lascars, by their hue and dress. Here, in similar clothing and with a made up face, the man chose his moment to approach the dray as the two lascars bore their cargo, crated up in heavy tea chests, under an archway formed by a freshly painted sign—The Monsoon Tea Company—that had been prominently fixed to the side of the adjoining building.

Slipping a jemmy from the folds of his loosely-fitting silk tunic, the man hastily prised loose the lid of the nearest chest, tugging it upwards to give access to the contents. Shifting the straw packing aside, he drew out a small brick-shaped packet wrapped in brown greaseproof paper. Resealing the box, he returned the jemmy, along with his prize, into the folds of his tunic before circling the dray and boldly returning, without a backward glance, to the side street from whence he came. Retrieving his hat and coat, he briskly continued away from the scene of his crime, making good his getaway.

*** 

To understand how these events transpired we need to step back to the previous evening, and to consider the nature of my relationship with Sherlock Holmes. While we are friends who have lodged together I am also, first and foremost, a medical doctor. In this capacity I have had occasion to minister to my friend's needs. During our early years I had been determined to avoid any conflict of interest that might impinge upon our camaraderie, but I had come to surmise—and often dismiss—that Holmes might occasionally indulge in something a little stronger than alcohol or tobacco. As a singular and intensely focused individual I had no doubt that any variation in mood or focus could easily be attributed to his eccentricities, and so these suspicions had never given me any real cause for concern. During my time away from Baker Street I had maintained a personal interest in the perils of addiction through the pages of the *Lancet* and *Chambers Journal*, primarily to assist in the treatment and diagnosis of my patients.

It was not until his previous case—the death of Sir Bernard Howard—that my friend's languid indifference to anything but matters of research and deduction aroused concerns that his moods might have a darker origin. The peer's apparent suicide—by cut-throat razor—had been called into question because no murder weapon could be found. Unable to verify his improbable conclusion—that the man's throat had been cut from behind whilst sitting on the toilet—Holmes' frustrations mounted. Deciding to spend a little more time in his company—much to the irritation of Mrs Watson—I would spend the occasional evening in Baker Street where my observations became more direct. With Holmes under closer scrutiny, I considered the best course of action to be that of distraction. I had determined to acquire a ticket for the music hall, which I presented on an evening that I would be away on practice duties. He dismissed the suggestion and, while it is rare for me to be insistent in the face of his belligerence, there are times when I will brook no opposition.

The playbill was a short one, made up of variety acts that I hoped might pique my friend's interest. The top of the bill was shared by a Chinese magician performing levitations and what would come to be known as 'the bullet-catching trick', and by the performance of a Shakespeare sequence by the Fantoccini Fantasia—a troupe of mechanical marionettes. The final part of the performance—and that which had attracted me to the show—was the debut appearance of the featured child performer, 'The Infant Tartini', whose act included a turn as a lightning calculator and a violin performance that the showmen compared to one of the greatest baroque virtuosos of the age.

"These so-called child prodigies are usually talentless mimics gulled into repeating a single and over-practised show-piece to appease the voyeuristic perversions of the uncultured masses." Holmes had said dismissively. "It surprises me that this boy's show-piece will be the Devil's Trill Sonata, a singularly impossible work riddled with more double-trills and tremolos than any reputable performer would dare to attempt in public. To see a child strangle such a piece with an ill-tuned instrument is not something I look forward to, and yet the possibility that I may be confounded is worth the risk. You can rest assured that my mood will be dark by morning unless some miracle ensues."

So it was that—under doctor's orders—Sherlock Holmes was bundled into a cab bound for the London Pavilion on Shaftesbury Avenue.

# II. The Monsoon Flush

The habits of Sherlock Holmes are seldom certain, however carefully I might choose to observe them. The nature of our business is such that these observations are as accurate as I can maintain, covering his behaviour, his mannerisms, his deductions and, of course, his health. My notebook is my constant companion, and although I record these occurrences contemporaneously, I am not above seeking clarification when I feel it necessary. However, as a gambling man I am prone to playing the probabilities, and after his evening at the music hall it was my assumption that he would still be asleep at a quarter-to seven in the morning. Not wishing to disturb him, I stealthily made my way up the seventeen steps that led to his Baker Street apartment. Slipping off my coat and draping it over my arm, I cautiously unlocked the door, firmly pushing it inwards at the speed I had previously noted would minimise its occasional creak.

The room beyond was dim. Curtains were drawn across the window that looked down onto Baker Street, and the fire was cold. Seeing that Holmes' empty chair faced me, I breathed a sigh of relief, gently closing the door and turning to set my coat upon the rack beside it.

"A little early for you," said Holmes, making me start. "You haven't even collected the morning's paper."

"Holmes?" I scanned the room from left to right, eventually settling upon my old desk, which had been in my blind spot. There, my chair turned so that he might face me, sat my companion, his hair ungroomed and his dressing gown loosely tied. "What are you doing there?"

"Investigating, Watson. You are a creature of habit, are you not?"

"More so than you, it seems," said I, crossing to the curtain. Flooding our chambers with summer sunlight, I turned towards my friend in a desperate attempt to read his expression. He remained inscrutable. "I assumed that you would rise late this morning."

"Were I to rise late it might rob me of the opportunity to breakfast with you," he replied, reaching for the small bell that rested on the breakfast table. Ringing it to alert Mrs Hudson to our intentions, Holmes changed seats. "Besides, I wanted to thank you for the most wonderful evening. It may have started tediously, but

the last few acts were most notable, especially the Indian boy."

"Indeed? He was not so painful to hear then?"

"On the contrary. I have never seen such technical precision in one so young, and his versatility should have drawn comparisons with a young Vivaldi or Paganini. To waste such a performance on those unable to appreciate him was my only regret."

Pleased to see the lift in Holmes' spirits, I joined him at the table, where my attention was drawn to a slender folder that should have been locked away in my old desk drawer. I reserve such folders for medical notes in a somewhat desperate attempt to protect them from prying eyes.

"What are you doing with that?" I asked indignantly. "Those notes are private!"

Holmes looked at me with a hurt expression, but not with an ounce of guilt in his piercing eyes. Lifting the folder, he drew open the white binding string before slipping a magnifier from his pocket.

"Holmes..." I used my sternest voice in an attempt to dissuade him from proceeding. Instead it spurred him on and he commenced reading the file aloud.

"Today the subject exhibited a variety of symptoms that included fluctuations of judgement and the rapid formation and reversal of opinions and observations. Such inconstancy and absence of self-determining power was observable through inattentiveness, diffidence and incogitant behaviour. I believe that this may be have resulted from a recourse to strong stimulants, taken to allay those uneasy and frustrated sensations peculiar to his present condition. These ministrations would appear to have produced a degree of excitation in which irritable outbursts almost became outbursts of mania. I fear that this form of self-medication may endanger the equanimity of his moral feelings and mental faculties, and that the seeds of various disorders will be sown."

"I-I really must protest..." I stammered over his narrative.

"Really, Watson? The file has no name attached, and the date—just three days past—relates to an evening we spent in each other's company. Is it really necessary for me to deduce who 'the subject' might be? Had I not already worked it out my curiosity would not have been aroused."

"I have your best interests in mind."

"Of that I have no doubt. Last night's distraction was a much appreciated alternative to a night of lonely melancholia. I do wonder, though, whether the purpose of my

trip to the music hall was intended as a distraction of a different kind."

"I beg your pardon, I don't..."

"Come, come. The more you have to hide the more transparent you become, my friend. I trust that this morning's little adventure was also motivated by my best interests. I presume you intend to return the items you borrowed yesterday afternoon."

I was speechless. My duplicity was exposed.

"I knew you were up to something even before you presented me with the theatre ticket. From the moment that you arrived yesterday morning I could see that something troubled you. Your fidgeting and frowns were barely concealed, and there were several occasions where you made to speak, but then kept your counsel. At first I had put it down to this..." he waved the folder in the air "...but your inability to focus on anything but my welfare gave you away. You wanted me out of the way so that I would be unable to interfere. Quite why you would do this presented only two possibilities: that it was either a matter of your heart, or a matter of my health. As your behaviour has not shown the former to preoccupy your mind of late, I could only conclude that your overprotective nature must be a factor. To whit, you took it upon yourself to borrow one of my disguises, make yourself up as a lascar—you still have a smudge of my make-up on your collar—and investigate something you chose not to share with me."

"Holmes, I..."

"Your coat and hat bear traces of dirt but your shoes do not, suggesting that you stashed them, and the way you carry your coat suggests that you are attempting to conceal something beneath. An object that will confirm my hypothesis, perhaps?"

With a sigh, I set my coat aside and passed the purloined package to my companion. It was as he surmised, and I could offer no argument.

"One of your street Arabs paid a visit yesterday," I explained as he snatched the packet away, examining it with wildly animated eyes.

"Mullins," Holmes confirmed. "The climbing boy. That explains the traces of soot I found on the stair and on the rug yesterday. What did he have to say for himself, and why did you choose to conceal it from me?"

"He and a couple of other lads had been paid to clear out the flues of an empty factory in Chelsea. While he was busy in his duties the new tenant arrived—an Indian lady accompanied by a large entourage. Mullins overheard a conversation in which she discussed this morning's delivery, which she described as 'an infusion powerful enough to put all of England in its thrall'."

"Aha; and it is this delivery you intercepted?"

"Yes," I said sheepishly. "I followed your own example."

"Bravo, Watson! You did a splendid job. It is good to know that you would be prepared to commit a felony rather than cast the temptation of this 'infusion' before me. What did you think it was? Opiates? Powerful stimulants? Did you fear I might be tempted to misappropriate more than one of these for personal use?"

The cold regard with which he addressed me made my heart sink. His own methods might occasionally put the letter of the law behind the need for justice, but he was right. I had no reason to fear that he might steal for personal gain, and to do so on a mere suspicion was, with hindsight, unforgivable.

"I recovered the sample for you to research. Chemical analysis is not my speciality."

"Ah, yes, the sample. Shall we…?"

Holmes raised the packet to the daylight. Throughout our conversation he had been turning it in his hands, examining it with the magnifier, running his fingers across it, and sniffing it. Now he placed it squarely onto the table before him.

"You were lucky today, my friend. Your lascar disguise may have stood you in good stead, but would have failed on closer inspection."

"Oh? Why do you say that?"

"Did you have an opportunity to read the label?"

"Of course," I nodded. "Monsoon Tea. But *that* is like no tea I have ever seen."

"You're sure? In the north of India and on the slopes of the Himalayas they make bricks of tea, do they not?"

"So I understand, but the poorer villages use them as a sort of currency, not for drinking."

"And the men of those villages are *ghorkali*, not lascars. There is a superficial similarity, but they carry a distinctive weapon…"

"The *khukuri*, yes," I said, cursing myself for a fool. "I did serve with Gurkhas at my side in Afghanistan."

"Not these ghorkali, I'll warrant. My monograph on teas is quite overdue," he said, "but I have done some research in this matter. Tea bricks are formed in three ways. The tea is moistened and compressed, it is bound with flour and compressed, or else it is bound with powdered manure and compressed. In the case of this brick the smell of a dark Nepali tea is unmistakable, as is the manure."

"So it can't be digestible then."

"On the contrary, Watson, the best tea bricks are bound together

with manure. See here." Breaking the seal, Holmes exposed the block of compressed vegetation. "There is a raised stamp, the maker's mark, which identifies the plantation from whence the brick has come. I'll need to investigate that."

Breaking off a pinch of the tea, he ground it into his palm, again looking with the magnifier before tentatively dipping the tip of his tongue into the concoction.

"Holmes..." I protested, warily.

"It's alright Watson, it appears to be tea. Monsoon flush, harvested in the rainy season. Dried tips rather than fannings, but it appears to be resined, which suggests a fourth brick-making process. Given that the Monsoon Tea Company blatantly sponsored two of the acts during my trip to the London Pavilion, I would venture that this is the infusion that your Indian lady believed would be popular with the English palate."

"What?"

"Let's have a cup, shall we?" He said with a low laugh. "Mrs Hudson shall be bringing the breakfast at any moment."

# III. The Sweep's Boy

From the pen of Sherlock Holmes:

It is not my habit to recount my own experiences, relying as I do upon the literary talents of my friend Dr Watson. Circumstances, however, require that I take up the pen to conclude these matters, for neither he—nor I—are able to rely upon our usually precise and reliable notes. I am forced, instead to turn to my memory of those events, overshadowed as they are by the spectre of susceptibility.

While the circumstances of our collapse are vague, I do recall some degree of confusion as I stirred from a catatonic haze. Blinking rapidly to clear my thoughts, I became aware that the concerned face of Mrs Hudson, accompanied by the boy, Billy, filled my vision. As alertness returned, I sprang from my seat, simultaneously checking my fob whilst noting that my friend was sprawled, face-down, across the breakfast table, his teacup knocked aside to form a dark stain in the tablecloth. It was a quarter to eight.

"Watson?" I circled the table to elicit a response, raising his head to check for pulse and respiration.

"He is fine," I concluded for Mrs Hudson's benefit, "fetch whisky."

Checking Watson's eyes, I noted that the pupils were dilated, and took from his right hand pocket the small silver flask of smelling salts that he habitually kept there. As I attempted to restore him to wakefulness my mind raced, considering the possibilities.

"Boy," I addressed the page, "fetch Mullins, the sweep's lad. Immediately."

Watson groaned, his eyes blinking slowly, as Mrs Hudson returned with the spirit. Consuming it quickly I returned the glass and demanded another, this time for my friend. Helping him to his feet, I carefully led him over to the chaise longue, settling him down as Mrs Hudson handed him a charged glass. As he stirred, I cast my mind back to the previous evening's events. The early part of the playbill had been typical variety fare, and the illusionist—Foo, the Great Magician of the East—was of more than passing competence. His levitation trick was unremarkable, marred by his perpetual breathing of smoke and fire, but the bullet-catching trick was very well executed. I had wanted to

observe it for some time, not least because I can conceive of several practical applications that might be useful in my own line of work.

The master of ceremonies had gone to great lengths to prepare us for the final interlude of the evening, which had been several minutes longer than was typical. This, he explained to the audience, was courtesy of the Monsoon Tea Company, makers of 'the wonder of the age' whose properties included stimulation of the mind, restoration of the humours, and the gift of unparalleled concentration. Such blatant advertising was most out of character for the variety theatre, but the additional investment was proudly demonstrated when the curtains finally opened. The stage had been filled with a large mechanical box, which the signage proclaimed to be the Fantoccini Fantasia. I had been expecting some tired and badly maintained old 18th century clunker, but the puppet theatre was completely new and of a design that I had never seen before. Rather than strings the mechanical marionettes appeared to be connected to the box by flexible snakelike cables. These enabled precise movement of a kind that could, incredibly, emulate the movements of an experienced stage player. The Shakespearean piece—Hamlet's play within a play—

worked well, but the mechanics were far superior to the vocal qualities on display.

As the marionettes took their final bow, the mechanical theatre drew them back inside the box, and a side door opened to reveal—to great applause—'The Infant Tartini'. Obviously sharing the tea company's patronage, the boy's emergence from the mechanical theatre was complemented by his attire, dressed like some clockwork doll in Renaissance livery. The initial performance, on a rare and well-tuned Guarnerius, was of Vivaldi's *La Follia*, accompanied by music projected from within the box itself, rather than from the orchestra pit. At the end of the performance the boy's porcelain mask was removed and he stepped forward, launching into a spirited rendition of Paganini's Caprice No. 24 in A Minor. Distracted as I was by the performance, I could see that despite being made up to look Mediterranean he was, in fact, of Indian origin. The artificially pale complexion could not hide those dark eyes, and the hands had similarly been ignored. He appeared to be all of ten years old, but there was something about him that made me a voyeur, enthralled by his deft control of string and bow before he shifted pace and style to begin his

grand finale—Tartini's Violin Sonata in G minor. This, the so-called Devil's Trill, is such a complex work that the superstitious claim it to be the most human approximation of the devil's music, played to the composer during a nocturnal visit from Satan himself. To my mind, however, there is little that could be more pure in the art of violinistry.

At the end of this turn the boy addressed the audience in flawless English. Seeking volunteers, he proceeded to perform a variety of mathematical tricks at blinding speed. I was certainly unable to keep up with him, but the numbers were accurate and there was no sign of trickery. Finally, the boy asked a variety of random questions which enabled him to accurately calculate the days of people's birth. These calendrical calculations were also correct, although the formula for such a trick is a straightforward one.

*What, I pondered, was the connection between spectacular mechanistry, a musical savant and a Nepali tea company?*

The question stirred me from my reverie. An instant later I was crossing the room to consult my card index, where I quickly learned that I was dealing with no ordinary business. The owner was listed as Pasang Rani Rana, identified by Black's *Who's Who* as The Maharani or the Rani Rana. Sister to no less than the new Prime Minister of Nepal, she was rumoured to be the power behind the *coup d'etat* that brought him to power only two years earlier. Her family had previously deposed the Shah dynasty, bringing tyranny and corruption to Nepal, securing its independence from the British Raj. Could this be the woman responsible for our present discomfort?

"What...what happened?" Watson was *compos mentis* once more.

"The tea, Watson. It was as you suspected—a potent infusion. Unintentional, I think, as the tea was in its natural form while the branded product on general sale is pre-diluted and in glass bottles, but it warrants further investigation. How are you feeling?"

"Well enough, I think. How long was I—"

"Just shy of an hour. My superior tolerance must have lessened the effect for me, but the important thing is that you were right! My somewhat sceptical view of your conclusions was driven by hubris, and I apologise. Your medical expertise has hardly ever been in question, and I should have taken it at face value. For now, dear fellow, I should like you to rest—I'll send word to Mrs Watson. In the mean time, we've another trip to the Monsoon Tea factory and an

appointment with the Rani Rana to arrange and a chimney sweep to interview."

***

The boy Mullins was short for his age—barely four feet six at thirteen years old. In spite of Lord Shaftesbury's ban on child sweeps some twelve years earlier he had been illegally sold on to a master sweep at the age of nine, and the curvature in his gait made it clear that the law was being broken. Technically, such a boy can only assist in the operation of a mechanical sweeping machine, but in practice the narrow flues were where he plied his trade.

The tale he told me corresponded to Watson's brief summary, but included a much more detailed description of the factory layout and, upon further inquiry, an update on the work that he and the other boys had been doing.

"There's twelve flues in all," he explained, "and we allus try ter eke art the work as best we can. Nine flues are clear so far, wiv three to do. We shall finish the job two days 'ence."

"I see, and can these flues be cleared with a mechanical sweeper?"

"Most any flue can, though Master 'atton don't like to tell 'em if 'e can 'elp it."

This put an idea in my mind.

"Could you complete the flues today, if you had the equipment?"

"O' course guv'nor."

"Then I shall add the guinea to your fee, Mister Mullins, and I shall need a machine."

Spitting into the palm of his hand the young lad gave me a vigorous and sooty handshake before setting off to collect the requisite items. I, meanwhile, set about disguising myself as a Master Sweep while Watson rested in his old room. With my disguise complete, I played one of my usual tricks, entering the room and making lots of noise whilst pretending to assess the fireplace for sweeping. Roused from his sleep, my friend gave a start, demanding to know what was going on.

"Beg pardon, guv. Just checkin' fer soot," I said, drawing a wooden rod from out of the fireplace.

"Are we due? Where is Holmes?"

"Mister 'Olmes called me in to assess a job, sir," said I, maintaining a neutral expression. "'E took orf this mornin'. Said you was ter catch 'im up."

"Catch him up? But I don't know where he's gone."

"'E said you would, sir," I added as my poor friend rushed to pull himself together. He is, of habit, a meticulous dresser, and to see him run around the room blacking shoes and buttoning cuffs on the move

was more than I could take. With a hearty laugh I exposed my pretence, and the look on Watson's face as realisation dawned was as precious a moment as any I can remember.

***

We joined Mullins at the same street corner from whence, earlier that day, Watson had embarked upon his brief criminal career. True to his word, the boy had with him a couple of bags filled with the tools of his trade—rods, balls, brushes and rope. Instructing my friend to give us a half hour lead, the boy and I made our way to the tradesmen's entrance, where we were quickly escorted to a first storey room overlooking the main factory floor. There we were left to our own devices, giving me the opportunity to use our vantage point to survey the building—the main frontage was a three storey block devoted to management and administration, while the workshop area projected out to the gable end of the building, opening onto a large covered yard containing ingredients and stock. From where we stood, looking out of a small window in the first storey annex, I could see that the workspace was divided into two areas. The first, accessed from the gable door, involved the mixing, brewing and bottling of the tea, while the second, taking up two thirds of the area, was covered by a large canvas awning through which several brass steam-pipes protruded, all of which were connected to a single pipe which carried the condensation back down into the production area, presumably for the steam to be reprocessed *in situ*.

"Mullins, there must be a boiler down there, is there a chimney?"

The boy nodded. "They said it was new so didn't need lookin' at. Master 'atton wasn't best pleased sayin' 'e should take a look-see ter be sure it were safe."

"Excellent," I said, rubbing my hands at the opportunity to stray into uncharted areas. "You look busy with this flue while I take a short stroll."

# IV. Into the Tiger's Lair

While Holmes examined the inner workings of the tea factory, I had been charged with distraction. With my head finally clear of the dark tea's influence, I was to summon up all of the indignation—and ignorance—that had fuelled my earlier investigations, confronting the owner or, as Holmes had identified her, the Maharani, demanding to know her intentions.

Hammering sharply on the door, I was quick to present my card to the well-dressed man that greeted me. Whether a business secretary or butler I could not tell, for he wore a long, intricately embroidered *sherwani* coat of the Alighari style, which to my experiences would place him as an academic. He had dark, thinning hair and wore pince-nez spectacles which balanced precariously as he bowed in greeting and examined my card.

"Would you state your business, please, Doctor Watson?" he asked calmly.

"Of course. I am here to speak with the proprietor. To voice my concerns and to seek some answers."

"I see," he said. "I do not believe you have an appointment. It is unusual for us to receive visitors unannounced."

"I am sure that is so, and if necessary I shall be pleased to make an appointment. However, it would go well if I could speak with someone about your enterprise before I complete my article for the British Medical Journal."

"Article?" The man raised an inquiring eyebrow. "Might I enquire as to the nature of this article?"

"I have been engaged by the Dutch Society Against Quackery to investigate the often fraudulent claims made by the purveyors of proprietary medicines. As a relatively new entrant to the marketplace, your Monsoon Tea has been brought to my attention, and I am currently working with a skilled chemist to gather accurate analytical data about its composition and of the curative properties claimed by your advertising."

"I see. Please follow me."

He ushered me upstairs, to the top of a new mahogany staircase that still smelled of paint and fresh wood. Here he showed me into a reception room, disappearing into an adjoining room from which I was separated

by a large oak door. After four or five minutes, the door opened and the man invited me inside, where I found myself face-to-face with a large white tiger.

## From the pen of Sherlock Holmes:

Service stairs led me down into the factory's heart, bringing me close to a giant copper boiler enveloped by clouds of steam piped in from the canvassed section of the workshop. Here the high pressure steam percolated through the resined tea and into a series of cooling stills prior to bottling. All across the floor masked *ghorkali*—dressed in a white kurta and pajama combination—hurried busily between tasks. Each wore the distinctive curved *khurkuri* blade, sheathed but ready for action. Slipping through a draped opening in the canvas awning to my left, I found myself in another world. Stretched ahead of me in multiple rows were what looked, at first sight, like the floor of a cotton mill, with automated frames that resembled dobby looms, attached to long spinning cams powered by rows of magnetic solenoids. These, their output boosted by regularly spaced steam engines, powered the devices in a complex rhythm that left me in no doubt that they were operating in unison. There was no weaving—no threads or jennies or hooks—just the spinning, clicking, bobbing beat of a mechanical corpus dedicated to a single process. Unlike the production area there were no *ghorkali*—no people at all—and I was confident in my solitude, passing along the row before me, letting the thunderous applause of the machines overwhelm me as I pressed forwards, making my way towards the centre of the mechanical maze.

I knew, at the back of my mind, that I was looking at a fully automated Lovelace Mill—the ultimate expression of Babbage's analytical engines, made possible on a grand scale by joint investments by Her Majesty's Government and that of the Third Republic. According to my sources less than a dozen of these structures existed, and none of them were intended for commercial use. Pausing to examine the nearest of the machines, I could discern three important facts: first, that it was a genuine device—the embossed plates, written in French, confirmed that the components had been supplied by *Concordia*, the officially appointed manufacturer; second, that these devices were not just receiving instructions via the spinning cams or the looped punch-cards, but that they were also returning their calculations to

a central control point; and finally, that whatever its purpose, the array was not complete, with empty spaces set aside for additional components built into each frame.

Continuing forwards, I was startled to find that I had seen the control device before, only the previous evening. Here, at the heart of the mechanical maze, I stumbled upon the Fantoccini Fantasia. No, I realised, it was a replica. The mechanical theatre bore none of the signage or theatrical scroll-work of the version I had seen previously, and there was no means of moving the object in or out of the work-yard. As the differences became more apparent to me, I realised that the 'stage' area was instead occupied by an electromechanical chair surrounded by snake-like cables which radiated outwards and into the 'wings'. Here, embedded in the centre of the chair, was a small person. Bound into the seat by grips and cables, it had taken me a moment to realise that this person was a real, living boy, whom I had also seen before. The dark fingers, last seen fiddling like the very devil, were familiar to me, as were the equally dark eyes—it was 'The Infant Tartini'.

# V. Enter the Maharani

Fear almost overcame me as the savage beast locked its amber eyes with mine. It was a fully grown adult, some eight or nine feet long, and the unmistakeable white fur and black stripes filled me with awe. I had seen tigers before—at least one specimen larger than even this—but not at such a close distance. It was hard to draw my attention away from the creature as my hand moved toward the pocket where my service revolver rested. Then, in the periphery of my vision, I became aware that it was tethered, relaxing at the same moment that my nostrils identified the sweet, cloying perfume of its mistress.

She was amazingly tall for a woman, easily six feet, and her slenderness was exaggerated by the close, form-fitting green and gold saree that clung to her immodestly lithe body. The hair, held in perfection by a tight, jewel-encrusted tiara, was a lustrous black, framing her caramel skin and a pair of bright topaz eyes that were startlingly similar to those of her animal protector.

"Please..." the secretary guided me into the hefty leather guest chair set opposite the enormous desk upon which my hostess leaned casually. Struck dumb by the divine beauty of the vision that stood before me, I gratefully accepted the chair, my mind racing. With a deep breath I composed myself. All I needed to do was to keep calm, maintain my story, and bluff.

As I took in the room and its luxurious colonial splendour, the Maharani secured her pet on a casual sofa before taking the seat before me. As she did so, her secretary silently placed a cup of tea on the desk-top in front of me before making his exit from the room.

"Thank you," I said, unconsciously lifting the cup to my lips, "very kind of you."

As the steam struck my cheeks and the sweet aroma of the Monsoon tea reached my nostrils, I was suddenly reminded of what laid me low earlier in the day, returning the drink, untouched, to the table.

"Please," the Maharani said, glancing briefly at my card before returning her enchanting gaze in my direction, "Dr Watson, do consider yourself our guest here."

The words were polite, but I could not fail to detect an air of authority

to them—just enough to keep me on my guard, and to respond defensively.

"I do apologise for my somewhat bullish entrance, miss..."

"I am the Maharani Pasang Rani Rana," she said, nodding gracefully, "not a title that bears much scrutiny in your country, perhaps, but I am of royal blood in my own. There is no reason why you should have known this, so I shall dispense with the formalities. Samir tells me that you were quite forceful in making your presence known, and that you were demanding an audience prior to compiling an article about my company."

"Yes," I said, blushing slightly at the gentle rebuke. "I have been commissioned..."

"To investigate potential quackery, as I understand it, doctor."

"Well, yes. More to investigate your new tea than to pry into business matters..."

"The Monsoon Tea Company holds a royal charter. We are a trading company much like your own New East India Company, chartered by the King of Nepal to conduct business in this country. Unlike your own businesses, we do not have an unlimited supply of educated Englishmen to run the company, and I have therefore taken personal responsibility for the venture. Our licence to trade is in order, and our product is of the highest quality..."

"Yes, your product," I said, breaking free from her gaze and drawing out a pocketbook and pencil—it was a desperate attempt to regain the initiative, but one I felt was necessary if I was to keep a clear head. "Do you mind if I take notes? I understand that it is based on traditional Nepali tea?"

"Monsoon flush," she explained. Her voice had taken on a soothing, almost sensual quality as she began to explain the tea to me. "The darkest tips of the richest tea, harvested as late as the season allows. Once fermented we add an infusion of yak butter, fresh ginger and tulsi leaves before creating a rich resin of honey and beeswax. All natural products."

"Fermented, you say? So the tea is alcoholic?"

"Slightly, but it is diluted with fresh glacial water imported from Northern Europe."

"But that isn't all you add to the mixture, is it?" I added. "There is the dung, for starters."

The Maharani smiled, unperturbed. She did not even blink. "The powdered dung of the common tahr is used as a binding agent, but its diet is entirely harmless. Mountain vegetation is hardly a threat to the British constitution—indeed it is similar to that which you might find in saloop—and far more appealing

than pickled oysters, meowing pies or the hot blood of a slaughtered animal that some of your poor use to treat consumption."

"While many foodstuffs are unsavoury, your highness, it is not their palatability that I have been asked to question. It is the medicinal properties attributed to your tea."

"Advertising, you mean? In America they sell snake oil cure-alls from carriages, and in your newspapers I find all sorts of devices and cordials which make spurious claims about the efficacy of their application. Why are you coming to me with such questions? Is it, perhaps, because Nepal is independent of your Empire? Is this some trickery intended to prevent overseas competition? I shall go directly to the Board of Trade if that is the case..."

"No, no, dear lady," I protested, for she was clearly better at calling my bluff than I hers. "It is a matter of coincidence that your company should have been chosen. It is not a commercial matter, but a medical one. I have been asked to review your tea, working with a skilled chemical analyst to identify the ingredients and their quantities, and then to apply my medical knowledge to the claims made in your advertisements."

"Chemical analysis? Surely the test of a good tea is in the drinking?"

"Yes, well..." again those eyes held me in their thrall. I coughed politely. "I came here to seek confirmation of the ingredients prior to chemical analysis, and to learn if any medicinal compounds were included in the list. The purpose of the article is to demonstrate whether or not your medicinal claims are accurate."

"They are accurate in my homeland, Dr Watson. The Monsoon tea is merely an historic cordial fermented in large quantities and improved by industrial processes for enjoyment by a new customer base. I can assure you that the claims we make are entirely based upon centuries of manduction. If people want our product, who are we to deny them?"

"Indeed. And you can confirm that there are no further ingredients? Nothing that might be limited by the Pharmacy Act?"

"Such as?"

"Ergot. Potassium Cyanide. Opium. Strychnine. Arsenic?"

"No," her beautiful eyes narrowed, "of course not."

"And nothing that we in the medical profession might consider to be a powerful remedy best administered by a qualified pharmacist?"

"The herbs we use have various qualities. You are welcome to examine them at your leisure."

"You can be assured that I will, your highness."

"Excellent," she said, reaching for a small bell which she rang momentarily, "then I can bid you good day whilst Samir escorts you to the factory floor."

Moments later the door opened and the secretary—Samir—stepped into the room. He appeared agitated, and beckoned his mistress to consult with him. They spoke briefly, whispering so that I may not be a party to their conversation. She then turned to me and smiled. Her beauty was undeniable, but the coldness in her expression sent a chill through my bones.

"You will forgive me, Dr Watson, but Samir and I are needed elsewhere. Can you wait in the adjoining room?"

"Of course," I said, glancing nervously towards the savage beast whose eyes—like those of its mistress—had remained fixed upon me for the entirety of our interview. I was more than willing to hasten my exit, and could not but wonder if the matter they must attend to involved my friend. Gathering myself, I stepped out into the reception room, where the Maharani turned to offer me her hand. Shaking it, I looked directly into her eyes one more time and found myself, at last, overwhelmed.

***

## From the pen of Sherlock Holmes:

Upon close inspection I was certain that the Indian boy was held in some sort of trance, probably against his will. His attention appeared to be fixed on a rectangular tray into which a set of black and white squares shifted constantly before his eyes. Tugging the tray free of the clamps that held it in place, I noted how the boy's eyes followed it as I tossed it away. Then they rolled upwards, looking directly at me. As he did so, I noted the dilated pupils and the dulled response that confirmed my diagnosis.

Examining what I now believed to be restraints, I set about unfastening the child and releasing him from captivity. As I did this, my actions seemed to trigger a response from the theatrical box itself. The snake-like cables that radiated from beneath the chair flexed, and I could make out the distinct sound of clasps snapping open over the clicking din of the mechanical Mill that surrounded us. Looking to my left and right I saw that the cables were now untethered, slithering and coiling into action. At the end of each, as I had seen in the theatre, were small mechanical marionettes, each some two feet in height. Devoid of costumes they looked stark and

functional, with gripping jaws and flexible appendages that made them more automaton than mannequin. Swooping at me from all sides I counted six of the things, all focused on a single target: me.

Ducking aside as the first of my diminutive assailants swept past, I felt a glancing blow across my cheek. Rolling towards the side of the 'stage', I checked myself—it had drawn blood. A second attack quickly followed, and I was forced to feint, pulling off the stove-pipe hat that had formed part of my disguise and using it like a sack to cover the top half of the strange creature. Next I drew the sweep's scarf from around my neck, gripping it tightly in both hands as a third attack followed. This time I looped it around the puppet's neck in an attempt to decapitate it. When that failed, however, I twisted and knotted the scarf around its control cable, limiting its movement and rendering it—for now at least—harmless. By this time, however, the other marionettes had entwined themselves around my legs and lower torso as hands pinched and jaws bit, dragging me to the floor as I struggled to break free.

Reaching to my hip, I freed up the small iron ball that dangled from the rope looped around my body. Intended for lowering into chimneys to clear thick blockages, its weight reassured me that all was not lost as my fingers scrabbled to untie it. Had I reached a safe distance I could have unwound it and, perhaps, used it like a weighted lariat or bolas, but in the confines of the mechanical theatre a blunter purpose would suffice.

It took several crushing blows to still the first of the monstrosities, and several more to force the withdrawal of its fellows as I inflicted serious harm to their extremities, even creating a kink in one of the control cables. This was enough for me to step away from the contraption, but not before I clamped my hands around the wrist of 'The Infant Tartini', and pulled him free.

Dragging the boy along beside me, I hastily retraced my steps, heading through the Lovelace Mill and out from beneath the canvas awning. At the foot of the stairs I called up to Mullins, whose head appeared a moment later. Here, with the promise of an additional guinea, I set him a new task and agreed that it would be best if he made good his own escape. Meanwhile, the Indian boy and I would take our chances on the factory floor.

We got half-way towards the gable entrance when the report of a pistol was quickly followed by the bursting of a vat filled with boiling water to my right. At the same moment I felt the searing sting of the bullet, which had clipped the fabric of my raggedy attire and burned my skin. Ducking under the hissing steam that burst outwards, I turned to catch a glance of my pursuer. It was not, as I had suspected, an armed *ghorkali*, but rather a London doctor of my acquaintance.

"Watson?" I called, pausing momentarily, torn between effecting a further rescue or making good my escape. I chose the latter, pushing the boy ahead of me and plunging through disoriented factory workers. As we ran, one of their number set himself in my path, reaching for his sheathed *kukhuri*. Closing the distance between us, I struck the underside of his jaw with an uppercut driven by the full power of my forearm. As he toppled backwards I snatched up the loose blade before guiding the boy up onto the tea-pallets stacked against the factory's rear wall. A second bullet ricocheted off the wall as the boy and I scrambled over the top and landed on the canal tow path that lay beyond. Limping away—for I had suffered deep lacerations in my battle with the killer puppets—it was not long before we found sanctuary in the empty yard of another business.

Gathering my thoughts, I determined first to get the boy to safety. My disguise and my charge would hardly attract the attentions of a hansom, so I determined instead to double back onto the main road. Here, as I had observed before entering the building, was the very steam dray that Watson had robbed only hours earlier. Such a slow and boldly-liveried carriage had no need of security, and had been left unattended at the roadside. I was relieved to find it fitted with a flash boiler that still ran hot, and hastily bundled the boy into the driver's cab. I then fired up the dray before taking the wheel. Precious moments passed, but nobody left the building before we had built up a head of steam. We were already a good distance along the road when our pursuers appeared, but by then the dray was too swift for men on foot to follow.

I took us north-east, passing from Chelsea into Belgravia, where I abandoned the dray. I had no bolt holes in this part of the city, instead leading the boy through the backstreets of Westminster and onto the Mall. From here we entered Carlton Terrace, where I made use of the tradesmen's entrance that led into the rear of the Diogenes Club. While it may contradict Dr Watson's accounts, this is my preferred method of entry, used on such occasions that formality must be circumvented. Escorted inside by Hubert, the head cook, I was able to give the rescued boy some food whilst tending to my wound and arranging for more suitable attire pending the arrival of my brother. Despite his surreptitious calling, the habits of Mycroft are singularly inflexible and I therefore had no need to enquire as to his availability. With my face cleaned of soot I joined the boy at the kitchen table. He was busy tucking into a plate of bread and jam sandwiches, his eyes animated and giving each part of the room a darting glance.

"My name is Sherlock Holmes, and you are...?"

"I am Aadesh Rana."

*Rana*? That the boy might be a blood relative of the Maharani seemed unlikely. His silence during the latter half of our retreat and his compliant demeanour eschewed a privileged education, and the nature of his performance marked him as an autodidact. Furthermore, the circumstances of his incarceration had led me to conclude he had been a servant rather than a master. The most probable solution was that the boy was a pawn slave. Debt bondage was common in India, so of course it was just as likely in Nepal. The only thing I could not account for was the perfect English accent.

"Where were you educated?" I asked bluntly, keen to get at the truth of the matter. Without Watson by my side I have little need for explanations.

"I do not appreciate being taken captive against my will. Nor do I respond well to coercion."

"I see. You will surely understand that you are no longer a prisoner, and that my actions were intended to release you from captivity. When I found you, you were bound and drugged—are you suggesting this was a voluntary condition?"

"It is an arrangement I entered into freely, sir," said the boy. By choosing his words with great care he had inadvertently confirmed his status.

"You are, what? Ten years old? The Child Labour Act was created to make such indentures illegal."

"I am not a citizen of Great Britain, Mr Holmes."

"Which is why I enquired as to your education. You are clearly self-taught in the disciplines of music and calculus, but it is your diction that confounds me. It is too precise to be self-taught and has none of the colloquial features I would expect from a non-native teacher. It also lacks the methodical bias that I would expect from time spent with an English teacher."

"My education was provided in person, by the Maharani," he explained. A compound education made sense, but personal tuition from the Rani herself rather than from a governess—was unexpected. "All that I can tell you is that my

father was an Englishman, so I had the basics of the language as a boy."

"An English father? That would make you subject to our laws, after all."

"If," the boy smiled, clearly enjoying the to-and-fro of our conversation, "you can prove my father's identity."

"Should that become the focus of my enquiries," I assured him, "that will present little difficulty."

"Difficulty, brother mine, is your bread and butter," said Mycroft as he entered the room. His large bulk filled the doorway, and the napkin clutched in his left hand made the deduction that I had interrupted a meal quite redundant.

"Ah, Mycroft. It would seem that I may have caused a minor diplomatic incident."

"The Maharani Rani Rana seems to think so," he said, unperturbed by my arrival.

"New travels too fast these days."

"Especially when I am dining with a member of the Board of Trade. The lady is making some pretty lurid accusations about your friend Watson," he said, glancing towards Aadesh. "Am I to understand that you've added kidnapping to the charges?"

"Nothing so dramatic. The boy came willingly. How is Watson?"

"The Maharani has give her

assurances that he is well, but will not permit him to be taken into custody until the matter is investigated. Apparently he discharged a firearm following a confrontation at the factory. "

"That should be an easy matter to resolve. I will testify that the shot was aimed at me, and that I do not wish to press any charge."

"Your word against that of the Maharani? What of your act of trespass?"

"I am certain that any such misdemeanour can be mitigated by my testimony."

Mycroft coughed, excusing us and leading me rather forcefully by the elbow, into the larder. Closing the door so that we were alone, my brother regarded me testily.

"It troubles me when our business overlaps," he whispered, mindful that the boy should not overhear our conversation. "Ever since the Kot massacre of '46 the Rana Dynasty of Nepal has been the devil to deal with. Harsh, tyrannical and unreasonable; but for all of that they have been passionately pro-British. Even the Maharani's trade mission is part of an attempt to reconcile themselves following tensions with the East Indias."

"Tensions?"

"With limitations on recruiting from the regular army, the New East

India Company is forced to recruit more natives. Their preference is for the Ghurka, but Nepal's Prime Minister objected. The Maharani is here to negotiate a deal, but her plans would appear to have been sabotaged."

The East Indias. It made sense—the company had nearly lost its Royal Charter in the wake of the Indian Sepoy Mutiny of '57, and regulations had tightened forcing a more aggressive expansion. The new Board had included the recently deceased Sir Bernard Howard. Dismissing my suspicions concerning a fellow board member, I realised that a mechanical assassin only two feet tall could easily have been responsible.

"Murder may already have been committed by one of these monstrosities," I said, entering into a full account. First I recounted my investigation into Sir Bernard's death, of which my brother was acutely aware. I then described more recent events in meticulous detail, sparing nothing so that Mycroft might be fully apprised of the situation. He listened intently, with little more than a raised eyebrow to give away those points that were of interest to him.

"Your friend's paranoia seems to have been well-placed," he said at last. "The Lovelace Mill is a trade secret freely shared with other nations, and *Concordia* are at liberty to supply components to whomsoever they choose—but only, as you say, for commercial purposes. I confess the use of stage puppets as assassins is a novel variation—it is not the first thing that I would choose to do with such technology."

"Theatrics do seem to be the order of the day," I agreed, "but the Indian boy and this intoxicating tea remain a mystery."

"The tea trade is still big business, and any deal to supply the Empire has considerable value. Thinking engines are uniquely placed for keeping track of the Stock Exchange, and that is the primary purpose I would expect to see. If this were regular tea I might understand the investment as a means of underpinning a shrewd bargain, but unless their venture in selling a cordial made from cold fermented tea proves monumentally successful, I cannot see it paying dividends. Besides, Great Britain has far too many people for large-scale mesmerism to work..."

"What of Nepal? The tea will already be palatable there."

Mycroft shrugged. "It is quite an unwieldy way to stay in power, but they do not need to control all of the people all of the time."

"Of course. We must act quickly to close this down."

"No, Sherlock. This is my area of

expertise. I shall secure Dr Watson's release tomorrow and arrange for him to be returned to you unharmed."

"And the boy Aadesh? He cannot be returned," I said, though the consequences pained me, "even if it means leaving Watson in the Maharani's care a little longer. Her plans cannot proceed without his mind."

"I can tell you haven't met her," said Mycroft. "As I am sure Dr Watson will attest, the woman has a singular intellect. She is more than capable of carrying out her plans without the aid of a gifted child."

"Perhaps. I shall keep the boy with me until Watson is returned.

Meanwhile, I shall see if I cannot get to the bottom of this matter."

"I will not be your accomplice, Sherlock. I will give warning to the East Indias' Court of Directors and set a man to watch over Baker Street, but without conclusive proof my options are limited."

"There is no need for a bodyguard," I sighed. "This evening I shall be focused upon research"

Mycroft raised a sceptical eyebrow. "I need your word that you shall not return to the tea factory to effect a rescue of your own."

"Very well," I lied, "but if anything happens to Watson, you cannot expect me to stand on the sidelines."

# VI. The Assassination Game

For the second time that day my mind emerged from a dense delusional fog. I found myself in a bare room, made vast by my distorted senses, its flickering gas light—blood red to my addled perception—casting dark and menacing shadows over and around me. I struggled to grasp the bed on which I lay, wrestling as I cast my eyes wildly around the room in a desperate attempt to ward off the menace imposed by the room's only other occupant. It may have just been a wooden chair, but to me it seemed alive, angry, waiting to pounce on me the moment that I propped myself up and rolled inelegantly onto the floor. Fiery pins pricked my skin, sending burning sensations through my body as my feet touched the floor and the noises from outside invaded the space between my ears. Metallic, echoing sounds that shattered my focus so my screams joined them, hollow and distorted as strange visions filled my thoughts. I had seen Holmes, but not as I knew him. He had looked devilish, his body outlined by an aura of black ash whilst his eyes had shone with a white brilliance that made my skin smoulder. A calming voice had pulled my thoughts together, guiding my hand to my pocket and my service revolver to take aim. The devilish Holmes had fled, but not before the thunderous boom of my pistol made the air around me ripple as a bullet crashed into its sulphurous hide.

"Holmes!" The scream erupted not once, but a dozen times, like a lunatic's repeating mantra as I rocked back and forth. That I remember the incident so vividly is a testament to how real it had felt. My ravings soon attracted the metallic footsteps and in moments the man I knew as Samir had entered the room, supported by two large and powerful *ghorkali* standing ready to restrain me. Blind panic overwhelmed me as I raised my arms to ward them off, but as I did so that voice becalmed my troubled humour. The Maharani, her beautiful and exotic eyes consuming my attention, had entered silently behind. Entranced by her soothing words I offered no resistance as the tip of a silver hypodermic broke my skin.

## From the pen of Sherlock Holmes:

My return to Baker Street was later than expected, and with the boy Aadesh in tow. Something had been troubling me during our brief journey back from the Mill. The boy did not seem like an assassin, and yet the present theory was that his was the directing mind that would guide the fantoccini on their murderous mission.

"Tell me more about the mechanical puppets," I had asked during our journey.

"They are just the tools of our performances. Machines, nothing more. They can only do what the code tells them. The codes are generated by the thinking engine before being relayed to me. I am required to observe and to make adjustments whenever there is an input error."

"What sort of adjustments?"

"Occasionally the Mill makes grammatical errors. By reading the code I can see these where a machine cannot—without me the fantoccini would be more likely to act incorrectly."

"Like attacking me as I released you from your bonds?"

The boy looked puzzled. "Some actions are pre-coded and I have no control."

"Of course. They can only do what the code tells them. Tell me, Aadesh, were you aware that that was happening?"

"Vaguely. When I am connected to the control box I am in a trance."

"So they use drugs to make you do things against your will?"

"No. There is no drug."

"I observed your behaviour intimately. You were in a hypnagogic state of consciousness, neither awake nor asleep. In my experience, unless you observe and amend codes in your sleep, it was an induced state, either through drugs, mesmerism, or a combination of the two."

"There is no drug, just tea and meditation."

"Then you and I shall examine the tea together."

Our conversation was interrupted by the cab's arrival at Baker Street. I ushered the boy outside and up the steps to 221b. Here I was surprised to find the door unlocked. A brief examination showed no sign of forced entry. Cursing myself for dismissing Mycroft's offer of a watcher, I kept the boy behind me and carefully pushed the door open.

Examining the hallway, I could see nothing had been disturbed downstairs. Turning my attention to the stairwell, I again saw no tell-tale signs. Cautiously I made my way up the steps, alternating my attention between the bannister, balustrade and landing. As I did so, I heard an unmistakable slow ticking sound above me, a tell-tale sound that was not entirely unexpected. Following the sound my eyes came to settle

upon a pair of legs—Watson's—standing motionless outside my apartment door. That moment of involuntary elation at seeing my friend almost distracted me from the danger that I knew accompanied him. There was no service revolver this time, just a blank gaze which looked right through me, and a pair of reflective mechanical eyes that stared from within the folds of his coat.

The puppet leaped.

In its brutal, most basic form, the fantoccini looked less like a human puppet and more like a scuttling four-legged spider. The limbs, like the cable to which the puppets had previously been attached, were snakelike and unjointed. The absence of any controlling device was unexpected, and caused me to cast a suspicious glance in the direction of the Indian boy even as I ducked and retreated down the steps.

Crashing into the wall, the creature clung to its surface, carving deep gouges in the plasterwork with a metallic *skritch* as it reoriented itself to look directly at me. It was not like those puppets I had previously battled—this model was armed with slashing blades and stabbing spikes purposely designed to do harm to a man. As the device paused, I became aware of the faint ticking sound once more. It was faster this time, but it gave me a clue as to how I should defeat it.

"Move!" I commanded, retreating further as the boy backed out on to Baker Street. As I did so, it leaped again, my face its target of choice. On this occasion, at closer quarters and with no props to assist me, I threw myself sideways and over the bannister, landing firmly on the chequered tiles of the corridor that led towards Mrs Hudson's accommodation.

The puppet landed hard before scuttling around and again fixing itself upon me. The ticking had slowed perceptibly, but the creation was just as fast as before, charging me fixedly as I reached to my right and gripped the handle to the small door that led into the cupboard under the stairs. As it propelled itself towards me I swung open the door, catching the puppet squarely with it before slamming it shut and holding it fast.

"Boy," I called out. "Hurry, there are railings outside—the fourth one to the left hand side is loose and can be removed with a good tug. Bring it."

To my right I heard the *skritching* sound again. Glancing down I could see an inch of blade-like fingertip protruding through the wood, unable to move. The puppet, I concluded, must operate with clockwork, and as such it would be active for only a short time. I had hoped its clashes with the wall and floor might have shocked the mechanism into stopping, but that ploy had failed. The cupboard, however, was secure, and with no escape the creature would soon wind down.

When the boy returned with the metal rail, I used it to prop the cupboard shut before seeking out Billy and Mrs Hudson to ensure they did not disturb it. With that done, the boy and I made our way back upstairs, where Watson stood, as motionless as before, as entranced as when he had shot me.

# VI. An Appointment with Danger

I had been left to sleep off my malaise, and as before I had woken to sounds and visions that fuelled my anxiety. Lying awake for almost an hour, my susceptibility finally abated and I was able to rise, surveying my surroundings as I did so. My friend had chosen to settle me on the chaise longue, within easy reach of a steaming pot of coffee and a large plate of sandwiches to which I helped myself eagerly.

"Ah, Watson, do join us."

Sherlock Holmes sat at the candle-lit chemistry bench, intently studying one of several test tubes that contained some of the tea fragments that I had acquired the morning—though it felt like days—before. A young Indian boy sat close by, assisting when required but, for the most part, watching intently.

"My analysis confirms most of what we already know. The tea is similar to Darjeeling, so I have no doubt that these are mould-fermented Monsoon flush tips. The dung most closely resembles wild goat with a diet of coarse mountain grass. Other ingredients include ginger, Holy Basil—or tulsi—used by Ayurvedic herbalists to make healing salves, yak butter and resin made from the honey and beeswax of the *apis cerana indica*—the Indian Bee."

"And that is all?"

"Not quite. As you know, bees make honey from the pollen of plants. One of the isolates in this honey is high in alkaloids. The sweetness of the honey counters the bitterness of the drug."

"Opium then?"

"It is possible, although my inclination is towards the *Solanum* family."

"Nightshade?"

"Or a close relative. Aadesh here," he indicated the boy, "described the local flora that surrounds the Maharani's palace. This information, plus the pinkish tinge of the resin, has informed my conclusion."

"I see; and this?"

At the end of the bench rested a mechanical contrivance that resembled nothing less than a dismembered automaton. Components were spread out across the table, tagged and meticulously recorded on several sheets of foolscap paper. The writing was unfamiliar.

"I have been cataloguing the form and function of the puppet," said the boy with a hint of pride in his voice. "Most of the parts correspond to

components identified in the book that Mister Holmes provided."

There, beneath the papers, lay a hefty volume. An engineering tome but with an ironic title '*The Evolution of Automata: The origin of the animated mechanism from impersonation to simulation to substitution*' by O. Sacker. I flipped idly through its pages as Holmes took up the explanation.

"These puppets are not mere clockwork toys, Watson. They are a miracle of modern engineering far beyond the dreams of Vaucanson or Droz. Tiny, flexible cables are operated by miniaturised cams whose function is determined by both direct and remote input that enables them to perform a number of functions independent of any further intervention."

My befuddled mind struggled to grasp the words.

"Are you saying this is one of those puppets from your night at the theatre? And this boy..."

"...is 'The Infant Tartini'. Quite so, Watson. I am glad you are up to speed."

***

In truth, it took Holmes another hour to fully explain the previous day's events, and of my unfortunate susceptibility to the Maharani's mesmerism. While he made light of my predicament, and of the injury he sustained at my unconscious hand. I had insisted upon checking his wound—it was a flesh wound that would leave little scarring—but it was enough to fill me with an intense feeling of responsibility. My amateur assumptions had drawn us into this nightmare, and my feebleness of mind and subsequent incapacity that had forced Holmes to press on unsupported.

I averted these thoughts by conducting a full medical examination of the boy, confirming that he was physically fit and sound of mind. In fact, outside of Holmes himself I had never seen such aptitude for intellectual tasks, which he ably demonstrated for us by taking up my friend's request to perform a rare and, to my untrained ears, rather frenzied violin solo. Sherlock took great pleasure in explaining that he had secured the score—which he referred to as one of Biber's 'lost mysteries—in payment for services to the Vatican. The boy's performance had an almost euphoric effect upon my friend, who closed his eyes whilst weaving his long fingers back and forth in time with the music.

With our interlude over, my friend sent Aadesh to continue with his cataloguing of puppet parts whilst he escorted me to his room.

"Watson," he said urgently, gathering his clothes together, "it is vitally important that you keep the boy occupied until noon. I have an appointment to keep with the Maharani, where we shall discuss terms."

"Terms?"

"Aadesh is a brilliant child, and quite devoid of any side or duplicity, and has accepted the evidence of his manipulation by the Maharani with good grace. While I may be forced to return him, I would rather make alternative arrangements. For this reason I need a good hour to parley. In the mean time you must keep him here, and do not set off until the clock has struck twelve. Then you must bring him—along with the police—to the factory. By then I hope to have brought matters to a satisfactory conclusion."

"I would rather have your back—" I began, but he waved my objection aside.

"You are too vulnerable at present. I cannot risk you being exposed to the Maharani's will again. Protect the boy."

As we spoke, I noted Holmes' choice of clothes was minimal, based upon the lascar disguise, but with a *kukhuri*. He took additional items from the sweep's kit that young Mullins had supplied. Over these he slipped an Inverness, concealing what lay beneath. As I opened my mouth to protest further, he raised his palm to cut me off once more.

"I have another appointment, which I insist you let me keep."

## From the pen of Sherlock Holmes:

My appointment with Mullins was brief and informative. I left with a sooty sketch of the factory floor plan and a small sack of Yale balls, which sweeps would occasionally use to see if a flue would draw smoke. It was still early, and the sun had yet to rise, so I was unobserved as I started to scale the factory exterior. Cautiously, I made my way to the rooftop where I found two smoking chimneys. Here, propping myself between the flues, I withdrew two of the chemical balls, dropping them down the smoking chimneys. I then loosened two tiles, which I used to cap the chimneys, forcing the smoke to return from whence it came. I then picked my way across the roof until I reached the rear of the building. As I lowered myself onto the sloped workshop roof, I heard the dull thump of the exploding smoke bombs.

Easing my way across the corrugated roof, I prised open the skylight set directly above the canvas awning that hid the Lovelace Mill from view. I had no doubt that Mycroft would take action soon enough, but I feared that his preference for diplomatic solutions would see the Mill gone before then. I noted that the machines beneath were ticking over like an engine waiting to be used, and I considered the risks. I could not be certain that I would not land on an active device, but the canvas looked sturdy. Pitching forwards, I spread myself wide as I fell onto the awning roof. It was a short drop of less than ten feet, and by displacing my weight I avoided falling through. The canopy buckled beneath me, but it held. I carefully unsheathed the *kukhuri*, cutting first a hole to see through, and then a U shaped cut large enough for me to pass through. Gripping it tightly, I dropped through the hole, feeling the canvas tear in a long strip, slowing my descent enough that I landed, comfortably, on my feet. Letting my eyes grow accustomed to the dim light of the Mill floor for a moment, I paused to separate the sounds of the Mill from the distant shouts of the *ghorkali* reacting to the smoke that billowed through the main building. With the sound confirmed I set off at a sprint through the Mill, rushing past the mechanical theatre and beyond. Here I paused by the boiler, locking down the pressure valves in the hope that the Lovelace Mill might prove a distraction of its own.

Checking my fob, I determined that it had been less than three minutes since the balls had been ignited by the fires below. Orders would soon be given to check the Mill and workshop. Passing through a narrow doorway into the rear of the main building, I plunged forwards, into the hallway and up the main staircase. As I ascended I could see the pandemonium unfold around me. *Ghorkali* milled around the waiting area, their great curved blades drawn as they fended off the great white tiger that swept among them. Watson had warned me of the beast, but it was meant to have been tethered, so I was uncertain as to why it was free and attacking its keepers as its mighty claws cleared a space in its desperate search for escape. Nothing had prepared me for the size and ferocity of the creature, nor for the remorse I felt at watching it tear and rend the flesh of the brave men that surrounded it. They were, I reminded myself, soldiers in the service of their princess, and the responsibility for the beast lay with her; but for each man that fell to its claws, a blade struck the creature, and its white pelt had already turned pink with a multitude of cuts.

Realising that that the stairwell would be its escape route, I pulled out my last Yale ball and a box of lucifers. Striking a match, I lit the

bomb, throwing it into the air just a second before it erupted into a star-shaped cloud overhead. Then, relying on the memorised layout, I plunged forward and to the right, avoiding the conflagration as I propelled myself through the door that led into the Maharani's suite.

The room beyond had barely been affected by the smoke, which I had intended for the opposite side of the building. A cursory inspection of the room told me that the tiger did not always reside here, and that the decision to transfer it to a place of safety had unforeseen consequences.

There were two figures in the room—the elegantly poised Maharani, whose attention seemed focused on various ledgers set before her, and her business secretary, whose arms were deep inside a large wooden cabinet. They were, I concluded, deciding what to keep and what to sacrifice.

"Samir!" The Maharani snapped, directing her assistant towards me.

The man turned from the task at hand, his knitted brows focusing on me as he set down the paperwork he was sifting through. Turning to confront me, I could see that he was armed with a small pistol, which was aimed squarely at my belly.

"Mr Sherlock Holmes," I believe, he said, his face composed.

"I sincerely hope it is my reputation that precedes me," I replied, turning to address his mistress. "It's bad enough you addled Dr Watson's mind, but if I find you extracted information against his will..."

"You will do what?" Samir barked. "The name of Dr Watson is synonymous with that of Sherlock Holmes."

"Really? I should not have expected it to be so well known in the Himalayas."

"You should have instructed your friend to use a different name—it would have saved him so much trouble."

"And spared you more."

"Coming here for a confrontation is hardly a sensible plan."

"I have done what I came to do," I shrugged, turning away from him to stare directly at the Maharani. Her sparkling amber eyes locked gaze with mine as I decided to test my resistance to her animal charms. "The confrontation is just a courtesy."

"It is alright, Samir, leave this to me," she said at last. "What is it, exactly, that you have done?"

Her diction was precise and without any trace of an accent. It mirrored that of the boy Aadesh perfectly.

"Your Mill is sabotaged and the properties of your vile tea exposed. Watson has been despatched to

bring the police to investigate all this smoke, and a representative of the British Government is investigating your plot to assassinate members of the New East India Company."

"Ah yes, our plot. And what is that exactly?"

"It took a while, but the *ghorkali* gave it away. The Royal Nepalese Army has been an ally of the British Empire since the Sepoy Mutiny, but the resurgence of the New East India Company—and its relentless recruitment of *ghorkali* as soldiers loyal to the Empress of India—has been an obvious source of irritation."

"An interesting notion," the Maharani smiled, "but what has that to do with me?"

"The Ghurkas receive their supplies from the British Army. Only a manufacturer based here can secure a supply contract, and those *ghorkali* drink tea, do they not? If you can undermine Watson's loyalty to me then even the loyalty of the famous Ghurkas can be weakened. You might persuade them to return to Kathmandu."

"As for my identity, I believe you know me because of my previous case. The murder of Sir Bernard Howard. Like many East India directors he had many Indian servants—making him an easy target for your mechanical assassins."

"I must congratulate you Mr Holmes, but even with proof I am immune to prosecution."

"Which makes it the perfect plan. It is I who should congratulate you, Maharani, but it ends now."

"Because your brother is a servant of the British Crown and knows everything that you know?"

"No, because you have taken liberties with my closest friend, and if you persist I shall oppose you with every fibre of my being. At present I amuse myself with domestic challenges, but I will happily embark upon a colonial career if I must— and my methods can be far from... diplomatic."

"I see. So it must end now because you are threatening me?"

"Better than if I were controlling your every move, like a puppet. There is little that disgusts me more than the abuse of power and the manipulation of the vulnerable. The idea that you would poison hundreds or thousands of men simply to weaken their resolve and bend them to your will is one of the most evil notions I have ever encountered."

Cold topaz eyes regarded me as she rose from behind her desk and closed the space between us until we were almost nose to nose.

"It is nothing to what I could do should I be so inclined," she said, exuding more menace than I had ever experienced. "You scorn me

at your peril, and if our paths cross again, Sherlock Holmes—and I suspect they shall—neither you nor Dr Watson will be so fortunate. This has been a costly venture, but I know when my losses must be cut. You will return the boy to me, and we will accede to your wishes."

At that moment, a mighty explosion tore through the lower floor of the building as the sabotaged boiler blew, doubtless wrecking much of the Lovelace Mill below us. As it did so, anger flashed in her eyes, and I pressed my advantage.

"I cannot do that, your highness," I said. "Aadesh tells me that his father was an Englishman, and if that is the case the Slavery Abolition Act is quite clear on the matter. I cannot in good conscience uphold a debtor's bond."

"Samir," she said through gritted teeth, "make arrangements for our departure."

With as much calm as I could muster, I nodded my own acknowledgement whilst noting the white knuckles of her clenched fists. This was not an angry woman, it was a furious one.

"Your friend Watson understands us better," she said. "He was in Afghanistan, I believe. Our people follow a code similar to the *pashtunwali*. You would do well to understand it. Nothing is forgotten."

\*\*\*

My departure from the front entrance of the Monsoon Tea Company coincided with the arrival of a fine MotoCarriage that bore, ironically, the coat of arms of the Honourable New East India Company. At the nearside window I recognised the formidable frame of my elder brother, whose eyes regarded me with a different kind of disapproval to that expressed by the Maharani.

"Good day, brother," I said with a cheery smile as he alighted from the vehicle.

"You gave me your word you would not interfere." "Watson returned last night," I explained. "Along with an assassin you are welcome to come and collect from Baker Street. I merely returned the compliment to the Maharani and sought her reassurance that she would pack up and go home."

"Do you know who I have in this carriage?" Mycroft asked.

I paused to consider. The livery was unmistakeable, and if there was a deal to be struck then only the most senior member of the Court of Directors could possibly be inside.

"I believe that I do," I said. "Can you pass on my apologies? Before the Maharani was implicated I had thought your companion as culpable as she in Sir Bernard's murder. It was an almost reckless error on my part, but I am sure Sir James will forgive me. Now, you'll have to excuse me as I am awaiting a carriage of my own. Oh, and I should tread carefully with the Maharani. Now may not be the best time for a meeting—there's a tiger on the loose."

# POSTSCRIPT

The case of the Indian boy who was not Indian, and the Intoxicating Tea that was neither intoxicating nor, strictly speaking, tea, is one that bears careful consideration. Dealing, as it does, with a reigning dynasty and an open murder case, I am reluctant to make it public. Similarly, the joint authorship of the tale bears a rewrite. Holmes gives away too many of his deductions, making the story more of an action adventure than a mystery, and the cursory reference to the death that started it all does my friend a disservice.

The Maharani is still at large, casting her wicked shadow across the northern states of the Indian subcontinent, and Holmes wisely keeps track of her movements in anticipation of reprisals. The *pashtunwali* code to which she referred is known as *badaal*, and is the inspiration for the phrase 'revenge is a dish best served cold'. We have no doubt that she will deliver upon her promise, although her somewhat strange sense of honour required that she provide a bursary for the Nepal boy's education. Aadesh is currently enrolled at a respectable boarding school in Hampshire, but maintains correspondence with my friend, who is already making plans for him to make a return visit to Baker Street in the autumn. They have already discussed an introduction to Wiggins and the other street Arabs, and with his brilliant and enquiring mind I am convinced that he will soon come to be known as the Baker Street Occasional.

JOHN H. WATSON M.D., 1888

# AUTHOR'S NOTE

In its original form, *The Moriarty Paradigm* was intended to be a series of mash-ups with no leeway for new stories. To some of us this presented both a continuity nightmare and a lost opportunity. For continuity, a series of mash-ups would necessitate introducing every new steampunk element through an original story, and some concepts need room to breathe. In a consistent alternative history it is easier to set up events through original short stories than by shoehorning them into steampunked mash-ups. Of course the lost opportunity is the ability to present new and original steampunk adventures that develop the characters of Holmes and Watson in the context of a richer and more personal world view.

*The Lavender Men* was deliberately commissioned to head off the idea of a steampunked Sherlock Holmes who fights off supernatural monsters. To us, at least, Holmes is better suited to a world of science and logic than to one where impossible magic and monsters hold sway. You can do a single story in which Holmes' familiar skills are overwhelmed by such things, but to make them commonplace renders him impotent to wonders of the spiritual world. This, perhaps, is why Sir Arthur Conan Doyle chose not to expose his hero to such matters, and also—perhaps—why he never entered the same world as Professor Challenger. The latter, however, is the archetypal steampunk hero, the outsider scientist whose obscure expertise pulls the mundane and the fantastical into the same stories, perhaps providing a template for adventures to come.

It is this template—that of pulp adventures—that Doyle himself embraced. While it is true that Holmes started out merely as a consulting detective, his sixty adventures were published over a period of forty years. In this time the detective genre in which Holmes existed evolved from one of gentlemanly pursuits into a world of two-fisted boys' own adventures. It has been argued that some of Doyle's own fiction—*The Valley of Fear* being one such example—were a major influence on the development of the hard-boiled detective genre, and the emergence of Holmes clones from Max Carados to Sexton Blake reflect this. One such clone, penned by Birmingham-born Arthur Sarsfield Ward (better known as Sax Rohmer) was the pairing of Sir Denis Nayland

Smith, Assistant Commissioner of Scotland Yard, and his companion Dr Petrie. These thinly disguised Holmes and Watson-a-likes were created as foils to the master criminal Fu Manchu who was himself an oriental re-imagining of the Napoleon of Crime himself, Professor Moriarty. With the more drawn out mysteries of Sayers and Christie filling the clever mystery niche, Doyle's fiction adapted, and by the time *The Case-Book of Sherlock Holmes* was published the great detective was inhabiting an ultra violent world where guns were used to shoot and pistol-whip with alacrity, and the fast-paced diesel-powered dime novel had replaced the gas-lit periodical.

This shift in tone was reflected by Holmes himself, whose fists became as important an element of his crime-solving as his brain. Does this mean he changed the way he conducts himself? Probably not. The younger Holmes would surely have had similar adventures had they been popular when he first appeared. One can assume that Watson was writing for an audience with more Victorian sensibilities, perhaps withholding the more graphic details which doubtless littered his friend's adventures. Original stories thus provide an opportunity to redress the balance, allowing Holmes to pit his wits and his muscle against a criminal underworld

that certainly existed in the Victorian period, but about which little was written. In the rarefied air of Victorian Society the slums of Whitechapel and Holborn were conveniently ignored, as were the horrors of war—despite Watson's service—and many of the conditions that social commentators like Dickens and Mayhew were keen to highlight.

*The Lavender Men* and *The Infant Tartini* are unashamedly pulp in style, eschewing the traditional detective mystery beloved of many Sherlockians in favour of a broader range of adventures that break the mould. In a steampunk world the wild frontier of America is all the closer, the threat of war in Europe all the more present, and the opportunities for criminal endeavour all the greater. Just as *The Lavender Men* is my attempt to do zombies properly, so *The Infant Tartini* is intended to introduce ongoing elements that could reappear in future adventures. Its plot could just as easily be that of a Doctor Who story, while its antagonist is very much in the mould of Fu Manchu's notorious daughter, Fah Lo Suee. While I can't guarantee she will return, I'd like to think she might have a few run ins with both Holmes and maybe even with his arch-nemesis, Professor Moriarty.

ADEM ROLFE, 2015
North of Watford

*A NOTE ON PLACEMENT*

As a volume of original stories, it is necessary for *The Lavender Men* and *The Infant Tartini* to sit between the events of *The Scoundrel of Bohemia* and the second story in chronological order. So what is that second story?

In the original canon there is one story that directly references *A Scandal in Bohemia*, and is set some weeks after the King of Bohemia has sent a 'reward' to Sherlock Holmes for his assistance in the earlier case. That story is *A Case of Identity*, which also references *The Sign of Four* as a recent case, which is said to take place in the month of September. This creates a gap between March and September in which earlier stories might fit, and consensus between Brad Keefauver's *Chronology Corner* and Baring-Gould's *The Annotated Sherlock Holmes* is that one other story fits into this gap: *The Greek Interpreter*.

There are therefore three events that concern us in placing these stories: the appearance of Mycroft Holmes in *The Infant Tartini*, the state of Watson's relationships (his recent marriage to one Mrs Watson and his meeting with Mary Morstan in *The Sign of Four*, and the nature of Watson's current relationship with Holmes.

First, Mycroft: While Holmes meets his brother in *The Infant Tartini*, Watson does not, and there is a negligible amount of time between the latter story and *The Greek Interpreter*. Both could have been written at the same time, and it is entirely possible that dealing with Mycroft in Tartini would be a catalyst for a more formal meeting between Holmes' brother and Dr. Watson.

Second, Watson's relationships: The nature of Watson's first marriage will be covered in our mash-up of *The Valley of Fear*, which precedes *The Scoundrel of Bohemia* by a couple of months. Needless to say Watson is married early in 1888 and remains so for several months prior to his meeting with Mary Morstan in September.

Finally, Watson's accommodation. We can be sure that his marriage is strained enough that it gets little mention during the stories set in the earlier part of 1888, but Watson has occasion to visit Baker Street from his Farringdon practice, and stays overnight when the occasion requires. *The Lavender Men* is therefore set in early June, with *The Infant Tartini* following a week or two later.

# INTRODUCING THE IRREGULARS
## by Adrian Middleton

With the introduction of Aadesh Rana, the 'Baker Street Occasional' we are opening up our world to a broader supporting cast than existed in the original stories. It is a tradition for new Irregulars to be invented in pastiches, having started with the American Irregular-cum-detective Harry Taxon, who supplanted Watson himself in many an unofficial publication.

The Baker Street Irregulars are seldom mentioned in the original Doyle canon, and their appearance diminishes as the stories progress. This reduction in appearance would seem to reflect the growing Victorian intolerance of child labour and its demand for better eduction. As acts limiting the use of child workers and improving the poor's access to education came into force, the opportunity for Holmes to call upon the help of children without drawing undue criticism was similarly limited.

The Irregulars are first introduced in *A Study in Scarlet*, where they appear as six bare-footed 'street Arabs' nominally led by a boy called Wiggins, who is the only one of the street Arabs named, and is presumably the boy most trusted by Holmes. Their role in this story is to act as the detective's eyes and ears, and in this role they successfully track down Jefferson Hope's cab.

The ranks of the group had swelled to twelve for their second appearance, in the novel *The Sign of Four*, where they again "go everywhere, see everything, overhear everyone", casting a surveillance net over London that succeeds in finding the steam launch Aurora.

In a later story, *The Crooked Man*, there is no mention of Wiggins or the Irregulars, but a small street Arab called Simpson is called upon to watch over Henry Wood. It is therefore assumed that in the intervening years, Wiggins has been replaced by Simpson as the leader of the Irregulars.

The final reference to the Irregulars, in *The Disappearance of Lady Frances Carfax*, a passing reference is made to the 'Baker Street division' which, added to the Irregulars' reach in *The Sign of Four*, strongly implies that their network clearly reaches farther and wider than the Marylebone district, suggesting that while Holmes has taken responsibility for organizing them, Wiggins (and later Simpson) must also play a role in extending the membership when required.

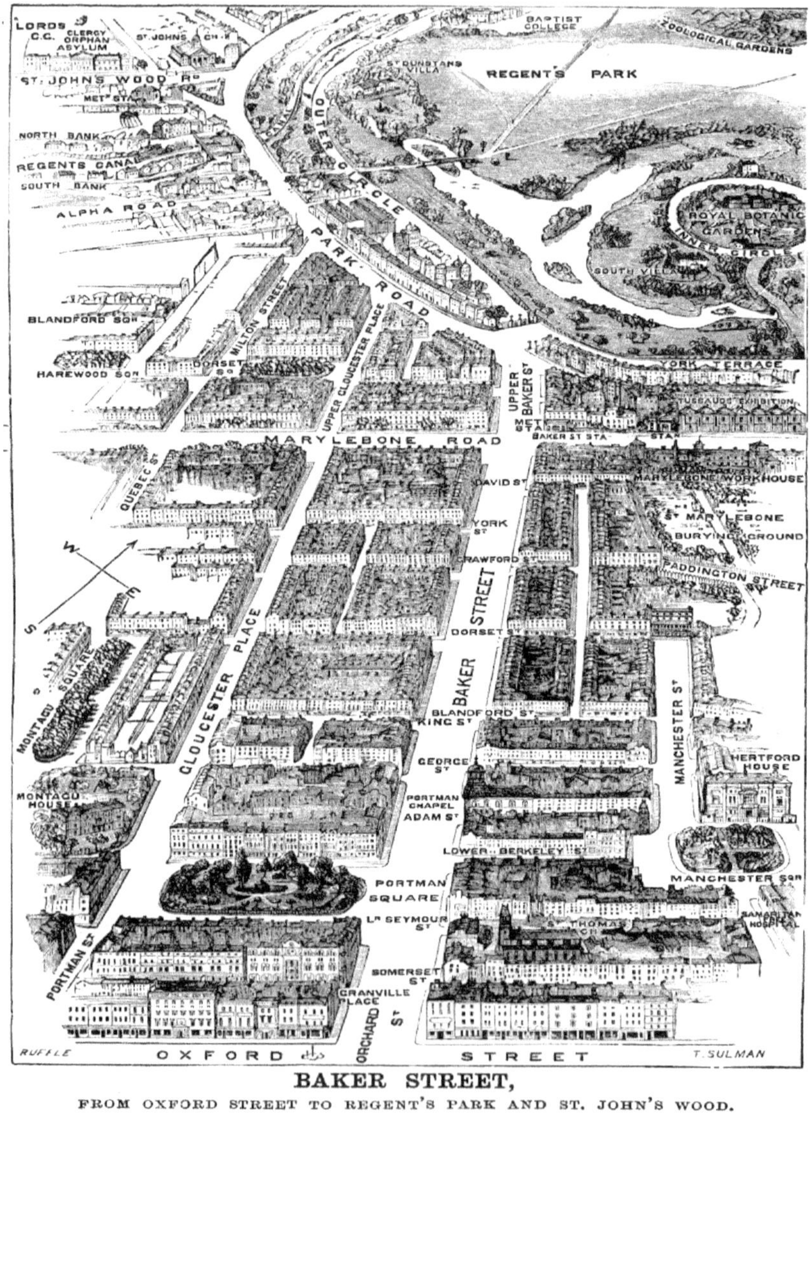

## BAKER STREET,
FROM OXFORD STREET TO REGENT'S PARK AND ST. JOHN'S WOOD.

\*\*\*

The term 'street Arabs' strongly implies that the Irregulars are urchins not employed in regular labour, and therefore able to be called upon by Holmes on a casual basis. Similarly their membership of the 'ragged class' of barefoot, black-faced children identifies them as being of the very poorest class. This would seem to be unlikely, however, as their affiliation with Baker Street itself suggests that the area immediately around Holmes' offices is where they are based. With Baker Street being a mix of commercial and residential properties well removed from the more familiar slums of London's East End, the would be very few itinerant street children for him to call upon. Also, when he introduces them in *A Study in Scarlet*, Holmes is clear to point out that there is more work to be got out of them than out of a dozen of the official force; hence they are not work-shy. Also, if the Irregulars were—as their name implies—children called upon to work for themselves or else carry out irregular work for one or more employers, then their connection to the area makes more sense.

They certainly could not be regular workers, for those in domestic service, factories and other full-time occupations would not only be better dressed, but also committed to twelve hour days and to lifestyles entirely associated with their masters. This would limit the work the irregulars might do to very few jobs, most of which would need to be based on the street itself, where the only possibility of employment is through shady gang-masters reminiscent of Dickens' Fagin. It is entirely possible that this is the case, but it would require some level of compensation to be paid to the boys' masters, and would draw too much attention to the role they play for their occasional employer. It is clear that Holmes' arrangement is with the boys themselves, paying them a shilling a day (plus expenses), plus a guinea prize for the one who found a vital clue.

On this basis, the following jobs are the most likely ones the Irregulars might perform within the environs of Baker Street:

**Cadgers and Dips:** While most common in the slums, the presence of street-beggars and pickpockets was ubiquitous across the city of London. While aggressive begging had been regulated against, any doorstep or street corner was fair game to these boys, who would often share crowded cellar accommodation, sharing their gains with their fellow tenants. As far as dipping was concerned, while Holmes may not have approved, his cases dealt exclusively with crimes involving those with money, and his familiarity with many criminal skills betrays a tolerance for the poor thief.

**Climbing Boys:** Small boys would often be kidnapped or indentured into the service of London's chimney sweeps in shocking conditions which led to high mortality rates among child sweeps. Resistance to the expense of 'humane sweeping machines' meant that regulation was required (in 1875) to licence chimney sweeps in an effort to phase out the use of young boys. In a steampunk world the skills of the climbing boy would be put to other uses (see Shimmies and Tappers).

**Crossing Sweepers:** Working for tips, these street sweepers would clear paths across dirty streets for those with fine clothes. Their principal duty in the age before steam was the cleaning up of horse-manure and dog-manure (called pure-finding, dog mess was a valuable resource for resale to tanners), which they could sell on for profit. With the dawn of steam and the rise of the MotoCar, the need for street-sweepers began to decline, and they would begin to switch to other duties (see Flaggers and Swipers).

**Errand Boys:** The catch-all term for fetching and carrying, most of London's street Arabs were ready and willing to act in this capacity, although establishing trust with a potential employer was an important consideration. The principal errand would have been the carrying of messages or the delivery of parcels, although when new technology is being installed or underground railways built, short-term work as tool boys to run errands for fitters and engineers became increasingly common.

**Mudlarks and Toshers:** Scavenging the mud-banks of the Thames at low tide in search of tradeable goods is a long tradition in the city of London, although with Baker Street having no river frontage, mud-larking would have been unlikely. The most popular parts of the river for mud-larking were where the sewers connected to them, and this led to a more dangerous trade: sewer-hunting, or toshing, which involved wading through London's sewers (of which Baker Street and its environs had plenty) in search of treasures (or 'tosh') which ranged from money dropped through sewer grates to the stripping of exposed pipes with scrap value. The practice was made illegal in 1840, and the improvements to the sewers by Bazalgette in 1865

made the practice less profitable, but also less dangerous.

**Newsboys:** The sale of newspapers on street-corners ballooned between the 1870s and the 1890s as the many newspapers competed both for custom and for pitches. As a residential and commercial district Baker Street would have been a popular area for such pitches to be set up and fought over, well into the next century.

**Rat-catchers:** Rat-catching was a common London occupation, using a combination of terriers, poison and traps to keep the rat population in check. One unexpected consequence of the trade was the rise of rat-fighting as a bloodsport, and the subsequent breeding of fancy rats.

**Shoe Blacks:** With so much dust and filth on the roads, shoe-blackers were starting to become a common sight on the streets of London, having migrated as a fashion from the streets of Paris. Like the more respectable trade of the barber, the shoe-shine boy had the best opportunity to discuss news and events with his clients, an invaluable opportunity for an Irregular.

So, with plenty of local opportunities for work—most of which didn't involve having a controlling 'master'

that might obstruct their work for Sherlock Holmes—the Irregulars could operate in sufficient numbers to be up to the task of assisting Holmes when needed.

Cue Moriarty. And social reform.

Even without Moriarty's intervention to make the Irregulars less effective, the improvement of Child labour and Education laws would certainly have diminished their effectiveness by the end of the nineteenth century.

The Factory Acts of the nineteenth century meant that child labour was prohibited for the under nines, limiting the hours they could work per day and per week. By 1901 it was illegal for a child under 12 to work. Similarly, between 1870 and 1893 the Elementary Education Acts made education for children compulsory until the age of thirteen. To accommodate factory owners compulsory education wasn't enforced until 1880, but it wasn't until 1891 that this education was made free.

Throughout London free charitable schools, known as Ragged Schools, pioneered the provision of free education for the 'poor or ragged', and it would have been to these schools—most probably the nearby Ogle Mews Ragged School—which the Irregulars would have, occasionally, attended. In practice, however, poor children would only

be compelled to attend if arrested and enrolled by the magistrate.

Holmes is likely to have either made philanthropic contributions to Ogle Mews or a similar Ragged School, or else have supported the new School Boards that were providing new elementary schooling. His use of the younger Irregulars would therefore have declined, although those over the age of thirteen would still have been of use to him.

Through Moriarty and the creation of a 'steampunk' Empire, new opportunities for the Irregulars would present themselves in the form of some alternative 'street Arab' occupations:

**Clockers:** Although most of the Irregulars were clearly ragged boys, over time a few may have emerged with better clothes and appearance. The well-dressed poor were known as natty boys, and the acquisition of one or two items 'of class' would have had a significant impact on their work opportunities. For example, possession of a watch would elevate a mere errand boy into a 'clocker', whose ability to deliver packages on time became a key feature, while a clocker with a bicycle would be even more sought after.

**Flaggers and Swipers:** With the replacement of the horse by the MotoCar, crossing sweepers could move quickly to address new opportunities. More motorized carriages meant that speed restrictions would be required in busy areas, and the assistance of a flag-bearing guide to walk ahead of the vehicle to clear a path and also assist in parking and manoeuvring in return for tips was a real earner. Similarly, with the humble windscreen wiper not developed until 1903 they would be in demand for the clearing of wind shields, as well as for the washing of MotoCars.

**Shimmies and Tappers:** With work in the chimneys all but washed up, climbing boys had new ventures to put their skills towards. As 'tappers' they could climb building exteriors, either to fit cables and transformers for new teslaphonic devices, and as shimmies they could ascend mooring masts and aerostat anchors to hook cables to aerostats.

Which brings me to the logistics.

Holmes works on flat terms with the Irregulars, who live in and around Baker Street, grifting and hustling for a living as they either avoid or embrace the opportunities of free education. That they can be summoned and can be ushered into 221b also tells us that Mrs Hudson and Billy the Page Boy must have some dealings with them. Presumably Mrs Hudson is kindly

towards them and no doubt throws errands their way as occasion allows, but it is Billy we must wonder about.

Brought into the Baker Street apartments to help Mrs Hudson, many Sherlockians have assumed that Billy and Wiggins may be one and the same—that the original Irregular became a member of the Holmes household—certainly the most popular first name chosen for Wiggins has been Bill or Billy. However, the evidence for this does not stack up, and Billy and Wiggins are clearly two distinct characters.

However, Billy's role as Page Boy includes the running of errands for Holmes and Mrs Hudson, and as a boy on Baker Street he certainly meets the criteria of being part of the Irregulars. Perhaps he was a member before we was hired? Whatever his back-story, Billy does seem to play a role as the link between Holmes and the Irregulars. Sent as errand boy to summon or confer with Wiggins, it is Billy who must leave Baker Street to be sure that the brain of Holmes can direct the eyes and ears of the Baker Street urchins.

# THE BAKER STREET
# BROADCAST

*The only place for readers of the Moriarty paradigm and other steampunk'd Sherlockians to come together and share their thoughts, both de profundis and in extremis.*

*Email: letters@fringeworks.co.u*

*www.facebook.com/moriartyparadigm*

*Second instalment, second Baker Street Broadcast. It's good to see that we have been lucky enough to receive more correspondence in an age of instantaneous, transient communication. The value of considered feedback is immeasurable, and for the time taken to give us your thoughts, we thank you. Now, to our first letter...*

I am quite taken with your approach to capturing the style of old periodicals and dime novels – the double columns and drop caps certainly evoke an earlier age, and the letters and crossword are very nostalgic. I confess the Moriarty Missive was extremely hard, and remains unfinished, although I think I have worked out the message [the solution is given elsewhere, and no, sadly there is no prize, but congratulations on getting it right – Ed.]. It seems a shame to fill it in in the book itself – perhaps you should give permission for it to be copied as a hint that we don't have to spoil it. The essays are similarly a nice touch (are there any guidelines for submissions, and what are the rates?), and quite informative—are there any other back-up features planned?

*Well, thanks. The essays tend to be put together by the authors of each volume or members of the editorial team. We'll happily accept articles that capture the spirit of what we do, but we would publish them like any old-style journal, as a reward for loyalty. The term No-Prize springs to mind, but that's probably copyrighted (so this will be our one-and-only passing reference until we come up with one of our own). We might throw in a free .PDF electronic of the issue containing the article, but our focus has to be on the work we commission. Regarding future features, the sky is the limit.*

*We'll consider analyses, essays, gadget/technology designs, comic strips, maps and diagrams. Anything goes really.*

As promised, here are my thoughts on The Scoundrel of Bohemia (I've heard of writers being chased for their stories, but never of readers being chased for their letters – until now!).

Up front, I do want to say that there really is no comparison between the kind of comedy mash-ups we are used to these days and what you are doing, and even though there is a difference in style, I didn't consciously feel the switch from Doyle to Middleton, and I was fully drawn into the new story as if it were part of the original canon. MotoCars and aerostats aside, the story could easily have been a straight Holmes tale, and I was taken with how everything that happens is a natural extension of the original story.

My one wobble was the similarity between the ending of Scoundrel and a scene from one of the Guy Ritchie films. That said, it worked better on the written page and felt more like a natural progression within the story than a stolen scene. It also allayed my one fear – that by extending the Irene Adler case her reputation as THE woman might be tarnished. Instead it was reaffirmed and reinforced. You managed to make Holmes a better detective than

in the original (Scandal was always one of his weaker outings) as well as making Irene more complex, stronger and more worthy of the epithet she is known by. Even better, Watson gets more limelight than we are used to, and is a better character for it. He has the heart, bravura and intelligence that he deserves, and for that I thank you.

Theatre of Judgement was very different. To see Moriarty without Holmes around is always a treat, and to give him a clergyman as a companion is quite clever, although I suspect the good Reverend won't be around for too long. I'm not yet convinced that the Professor has the capacity to be an anti-hero, but I'm willing to be convinced. This is certainly as good a start as any.

- Kaitlyn

*Yes, I confess, we chase those who say they might write us a letter. And it worked. It's very lonely here at Fringeworks Towers, waiting for the tumbleweed to roll past and for the clunk of fan mail in the letterbox. Even better, we now know that not only do we sell copies of our books, but also that people read them!*

*As grand experiments go, this format is really about rekindling something that existed before comic books, film serials and big budget movies— these are things that elevate our*

expectations, and which influence us all—consciously or unconsciously. The scene in question evolved naturally, and wasn't inspired by the Guy Ritchie film but, as his probably was, by the facts presented in the original story. If you're going to have a climactic scene involving a King and an Opera Singer, where else would you set it but at an operatic performance?

Professor Moriarty will be an occasional visitor to this series. Rest assured there will be others taking up the occasional limelight offered by our supporting stories. Whether he is an anti-hero or a villain remains to be seen—the road to hell is paved with good intentions, so it's equally possible that a selfish man might do good as a consequence of his evil intent.

I very much like the physical appearance of your new series, but I'm afraid my interest lies in the genius of the original format. I prefer to re-read the canon and to play the Game. I enjoy the occasional pastiche, but when it veers into science fiction or the supernatural I'm afraid it enters territory best served by other detectives. Good luck with your project, but I'm afraid its all too far fetched for me.

- A Lloyd

Given that you're already au fait with the difference between the original canon and steampunk, I'd say you don't need us. Obviously its sad that someone who takes the time to try us out doesn't find us to their taste, but that's no bad thing. Holmes patstiches are popular for a reason—the Holmes canon is probably the most scrutinized body of work outside of the Bible, the Koran and the works of Shakespeare, and for all of his genius Doyle's work is some of the easiest to emulate. It can (and has within these pages) be argued that many other mystery and detective stories were copying the methods established by Doyle without using the same characters. Similarly, moving Holmes beyond the context of the original stories and transplanting him into different genres is a very different animal to the traditional pastiche.

S tory concept for you if you'd like it: Sherlock Holmes and the Entrepreneur's Thumb...[Content omitted]. Feel free to use all or none of the above. I hereby give you all rights to it.

- Ben

Thanks, Ben. Its very flattering when we receive messages like this, but it can also be very dangerous. As it is we have another idea in mind for our mash-up of The Engineer's Thumb, when we get around to it, but it is important—particularly with work for hire—that we commission the story and the writer

together. We buy the talent and the idea, or else we pay the talent to flesh out an idea of our own. It is equally important that we read every pitch we are sent—which can take time—so that we can formally accept or reject it. Stories in limbo are an even scarier thing to deal with, and the age of social media just made things a whole lot worse.

I read Theatre of Judgement with real excitement. As a short story it ticked all my boxes, and it promises perhaps the most exciting take on Moriarty I've seen. I'm a big fan of the John Gardner books and also of the recently reprinted Michael Kurland adventures – they brought the professor out of the shadows to take centre stage, surrounding him with a cast of supporting characters. I trust you plan on doing the same.

One question – this seems to be a stand-alone universe, yet you share the same core concept as David Dvorkin's excellent Time for Sherlock Holmes. Is that a conscious choice or coincidence? And are you planning to let us play the game or are there plans to fill in the blanks?

- Andrew Foster

Blanks? They will definitely be filled in Andrew, but I can assure you that this isn't the same core concept. Time for Sherlock Holmes, as I recall, was

Holmes chasing Moriarty through time after the latter had stolen the Time Machine from H G Wells. As in the film Time after Time, where Wells is played by Malcolm McDowell, the author is himself the time traveller. That won't be the road we travel, and I doubt that the Game will easily reconcile what we have planned with what happened in Dvorkin's novel. I'm afraid you're going to have to watch this space.

As far as a supporting cast is concerned—yes, there are plans not just to flesh out the details of those who work with Holmes and Watson, but also to provide more insight into the Empire of the Napoleon of Time (see what we did there?).

This brings us to the following correspondence – part of a larger review shared with us in advance ad giving us some insight into how well the series is being received.

The Moriarty Paradigm is a concept that has been well realized, and it has created a world that will repay both the casual reader and the Holmes enthusiast The character of Sherlock Holmes has been captured accurately, and his mannerisms, deductions and modes of speech all preserved in a world where the Channel Tunnel has been built, the Mannheim-Benz roars and Lunar expeditions have taken place.

The Scoundrel in Bohemia can

be read and enjoyed as a stand alone novel within this multiverse. It interweaves Doyle's original text with naturally occurring steampunk elements and new text to create an integrated whole. With a surrounding cast of characters both original and new, Irene Adler —The Woman—is both familiar, yet reinvented: her timeline takes a different course in this world but remains believable. However, a prior reading of appendices in Eliminating the Possible may enable the reader to fully appreciate how the Holmes and steampunk elements have been integrated, and gain the most from their immersion in this multiverse.

The Moriarty Paradigm is highly recommended and this reader will be extremely interested to see how it develops over time.

- Angeline Sudworth

*Perhaps the greatest compliment we can get is to receive a positive review Angeline, and we're thrilled that you haven't just reviewed our first two releases, but also that you have shared them with us in advance so we can bask in the warmth of approval and appreciation. Even better, it is plain to see that we have hit the mark – your review pretty much tells us that we are on the right track, and that we have a good shot at achieving what we are setting out to do. Here's hoping that*

*we can go from strength to strength and, perhaps, start to exceed your expectations.*

Thoroughly enjoying the series so far. I am reminded by the premise of several Holmes/SF stories, particularly Isaac Asimov's The Ultimate Crime from his Black Widower stories, in which he revealed that Moriarty's Dynamics of an Asteroid provided evidence of the destruction of planet five (the surmised planet between Mars and Jupiter). The idea of a 'steampunk world' rooted in an SF-fuelled alternative history seems on step beyond anything that has gone before, and although The Scoundrel of Bohemia only helps to set the scene, the wholly original Theatre of Judgement provided a much starker introduction to what is going on, and to what I hope will become a dominant theme over time. As a reader of Doctor Who: The New Adventures back in the nineties, I was particularly amused by the veiled reference to Andy Lane's Library of St John the Beheaded from his Who-Holmes crossover novel All Consuming Fire.

- Steve Jones

*Ah, Steve, yes, the Doctor Who reference. We couldn't resist. Asimov, of course, was himself a Baker Street*

*Irregular, and the story you mentioned appeared in his collection More Tales of the Black Widowers – the widowers being a private dining club who shared tales of mystery over food, tobacco and fine wine. And even though our version of Dynamics of an Asteroid serves a slightly different purpose, it is entirely possible that it proved the existence of planet five as well. Wouldn't that be fun!*

I agree with Basil Huntingdon-Whyte (is that his real name? And as for Air Captain Jackstaff...): we need some cross-over fiction. That said, I am of the view that horror and the supernatural aren't appropriate directions for this to take. Holmes is a rationalist and to present the impossible on a continuing basis rather undermines his mindset. However, there are plenty of more subtle and less well-known characters whose adventurs might translate well into the world that Holmes inhabits. Guy Boothby's Dr Nikola, Grant Allen's Colonel Clay and of course Sax Rohmer's yellow peril himself, Dr Fu Manchu all fit in with the dark and foggy world that Holmes inhabits, and would be great assets to the series. Please think again about the possibilities.

- Janet Hammond

*Thanks, Janet, but we're adamant —at this stage—that we'd prefer to introduce original characters instead of established ones, although we will keep an open mind, and you're right that the more obscure and forgotten characters are more likely to make the cut should we change our minds. Fu Manchu, however, is most definitely off the table. There's always Cay Van Ash's excellent Ten Years Beyond Baker Street if you want that kind of cross-over, but as you will see from this volume we're already adding a pinch of Rohmer to our fiction, and I'm sure that the Maharani from our supporting story will be seen again at some point, perhaps as a recurring villainess as time goes by.*

# MORIARTY'S MISCHIEVOUS MISSIVE 2

*Professor Moriarty has again messaged his minions. Sherlock Holmes has identified which squares contain his latest set of instructions, but he needs your help to find and rearrange the letters.*

## Across

1 Mary Sutherland advertised for Hosmer Angel here.

4 A barren heath where mires may be found.

6 Scientist that studies or treats mental illness.

8 Where great detectives go to retire.

9 Possible name of Holmes' father.

10 Weighted leather weapon used by criminals.

13 Copper's informant.

14 Soporific substance.

18 We rely upon Watson's.

19 Father of the modern detective story.

20 Watson's paymaster.

21 Three of the four were of this sect.

22 Lens.

23 German revenge.

25 American detectives.

26 Holmes' method.

28 The Birlstone Butler.

29 Old Sherman's faithful detective.

31 Did the dog do anything in the night-time?

32 Skill shared by Holmes and Gillette.

33 Silver Blaze was to be made lame by nicking this.

35 Identity of the Speckled Band.

36 Hope's falling sickness.

37 Holmes briefly visited this French town.

## Down

1 Surgeon's assistant (Stamford had been Watson's).

2 Polyphonic motets of _____.

3 Five.

4 Steampunk vehicle from the Moriarty Paradigm.

5 Shh... final celeb car.

7 Holmes reviews it daily.

11 London Railway.

12 The Hebrons lived here.

13 Danish, Finnish, Icelandic, Norwegian or Swedish.

15 K.K.K. Family.

16 Head eel gear dude.

17 As made by Holmes' 18 across.

19 More than one of these was stolen from Woolwich Arsenal.

24 Town en route to Meiringen.

27 Suicide poison.

28 Lighter than air fuel and respiratory stimulant.

30 Last French Dynasty.

34 Langdale.

**Solution to Moriarty's Mischievous Missive #1: "Adler must be neutralized"**

**Across:** 1. Pawn shop; 4. Peerless; 7. Sewer; 9. Seven Per Cent; 11. CO; 12. Tutor; 13. Birmingham; 14. Northumberland; 17. Ormond Sacker; 21. Anatomy; 22. Milverton; 23. Door; 25. Baker Street; 27. Art; 28. Wells; 30. Irene Adler; 31. Horowitz; 32. Yellow.

**Down:** 1. Peter Haining; 2. Sepoys; 3. Prague; 5. Sholto; 6. Vernet; 8. Robert; 10. Elementary my dear Watson; 11. Carbuncle; 13. Billy; 15. Hand; 16. Flash; 18. Nemor; 19. Andaman; 20. Harry Taxon; 24. Aurora; 25. Seven; 29. School.

# CONTRIBUTORS

Martin Reimann: A Czech born, Belgium raised, Norwich University of the Arts graduate, Martin is primarily a games designer and artist whose memorable and quirky style imbues much of his work with a personality and character that reflects his multi national roots.

Adem Rolfe: A surrealist short storyteller with a passion for sabulous, science based, surrealist speculative stuff, Adem lives in the cold north where a fine wine, a well-knitted sweater and a good book keep him entertained as he looks longingly towards the northern lights.

Adrian Middleton: Writer, editor, publisher, local historian and the son of a real-life detective, Adrian is the creator of the Moriarty Paradigm, and when he isn't editing, he also writes original science fiction, fantasy and adventure stories.

# ENDNOTE

During their original run the Sherlock Holmes stories took little notice of real history. Events were of course reflected in some of the stories Doyle wrote, but the people involved were alive, and the truth behind events was often uncertain. While Doyle and Joseph Bell, the man upon whom he based Sherlock Holmes, were happy to write articles and offer opinions on such incidents, Holmes himself was kept at arms length.

Robert Knox, the inventor of the theory of transcendental anatomy, is best known for his involvement in the West Port Murders whose perpetrators – Burke and Hare – have become infamous as resurrectionists known as 'the bodysnatchers'. While the affair destroyed his career and saw him die in obscurity more than a decade before Doyle studied at the University of Edinburgh, his legacy cast a long shadow over the medical profession of the author's time.

While Doyle's account of Watson's time in Afghanistan was entirely fictional, it drew on his interest in military history and also on his contact with other doctors who did serve there. Although in the news less, Nepal was a hotbed of activity in the early days of the British Raj, from political coups to the supply of Ghurka mercenaries to the British Army of the time. Lurid tales of the most recent event – a military coup d'etat in 1885 – would have been a talking point among the medical personnel returning from tours of service in India at the time Doyle penned Holmes' early adventures.

Stripped of the sensitivities of the time we can use the benefit of hindsight to incorporate historical events into the stories we present, from the more public question of how Holmes would have dealt with Jack the Ripper to more intimate questions about the real-life public figures and events that might have impinged upon his life.

# MORIARTY PARADIGM

## ELIMINATING THE POSSIBLE
**ed. Adrian Middleton**

Imagine the richly detailed Victorian London of Sherlock Holmes reinvented as a steampunk world created by the criminal genius of his arch-nemesis, Professor James Moriarty. Airships. Ray Guns. Moonshots. Tesla. Time Machines. Welcome to The Moriarty paradigm. Eliminating the Possible uses a remarkable series of excerpts, articles and original fiction to provide the introduction to an entirely new Holmes canon. Filled with all the familiar tropes of the steampunk genre, the Moriarty paradigm brings together a number of modern writers to reintroduce readers to the mystery and adventures of Sherlock Holmes.

## THE YELLOW FAÇADE
**by Christer Van**

Who or what is that face that stares, livid, deadly yellow, and with something set and rigid about it, from an upstairs window? What connects it to the Phantom of the Pool of London? Can Sherlock Holmes and Doctor unravel the secret past of Mrs Grant Munro and the legacy of her first husband, John Hebron? Or will they fail to solve the mystery of the yellow facade?

## A STUDY IN STEAMPUNK
**by David A. McIntee**

Returning to London to recuperate from injuries sustained over Afghanistan, Dr John Watson's quest for new accommodation brings him face to face with the eccentric Mr Sherlock Holmes, and his consulting rooms at 221B Baker Street. Plunged into the world of the scientific method of detection, the physician finds that he has not, after all, left death and mayhem in his past. He soon finds himself embroiled in a murder mystery involving coded messages, Her Majesty's Aeronautical Service, and the ever-present shadow of Professor James Moriarty. With no shortage of suspects, and the best brains of Scotland Yard left baffled, it is up to the self-styled Consulting Detective, and the recuperating Surgeon-Lieutenant, to learn to work together in unravelling the politics of the People of the Clouds, and to bring to an end an invisible killer's reign of terror.

# FIND OUT MORE ABOUT FRINGEWORKS BY SCANNING THE QR CODE BELOW

WWW.FRINGEWORKS.CO.UK

www.ingramcontent.com/pod-product-compliance
Lightning Source LLC
Chambersburg PA
CBHW070630130626
46555CB00006B/2512